P9-DNO-035

Hoofbeats

Lara and the Moon-Colored Filly

Book Two

by KATHLEEN DUEY

DUTTON CHILDREN'S BOOKS
NEW YORK

DUTTON CHILDREN'S BOOKS
A division of Penguin Young Readers Group

Published by the Penguin Group
Penguin Young Readers Group, 345 Hudson Street,
New York, New York 10014, U.S.A.
Penguin Group (Canada), 10 Alcorn Avenue, Toronto, Ontario,
Canada M4V 3B2 (a division of Pearson Penguin Canada Inc.)
Penguin Books Ltd, 80 Strand, London WC2R 0RL, England
Penguin Ireland, 25 St Stephen's Green, Dublin 2, Ireland
(a division of Penguin Books Ltd)
Penguin Group (Australia), 250 Camberwell Road, Camberwell,
Victoria 3124, Australia (a division of Pearson Australia Group Pty Ltd)
Penguin Books India Pvt Ltd, 11 Community Centre,
Panchsheel Park, New Delhi - 110 017, India
Penguin Group (NZ), Cnr Airborne and Rosedale Roads, Albany, Auckland 1310, New Zealand (a division of Pearson New Zealand Ltd)
Penguin Books (South Africa) (Pty) Ltd, 24 Sturdee Avenue,
Rosebank, Johannesburg 2196, South Africa

Penguin Books Ltd, Registered Offices: 80 Strand,
London WC2R 0RL, England

LIBRARY OF CONGRESS CATALOGING-IN-PUBLICATION DATA

Duey, Kathleen.
Lara and the moon-colored filly / Kathleen Duey.
p. cm. — (Hoofbeats ; bk. 2)
Sequel to: Lara and the gray mare.
Summary: Captured by members of another Irish clan, Lara continues to protect
the young filly, Dannsair, and ponders how they might escape together.
ISBN 0-525-47333-5 (hardcover) — ISBN 0-14-240231-1 (pbk.)
[1. Horses—Fiction. 2. Ireland—History—Fiction.] I. Title. II. Series.
PZ7.D8694Lat 2005 [Fic]—dc22 2004024933

Published in the United States by Dutton Children's Books,
a division of Penguin Young Readers Group
345 Hudson Street, New York, New York 10014
www.penguin.com/youngreaders

Printed in USA • First Edition

1 3 5 7 9 10 8 6 4 2

For Star, a dapple gray Welsh Pony, with a true five-point white star on his side. He was the smartest pony I have ever known. I met him in a dark pasture, in a driving rain, on the night he was born. Birth is a fierce, joyous miracle. Anyone who falls in love with a newborn foal is permanently touched, forever changed, forever grateful.

Hoofbeats

Lara and the Moon-Colored Filly

CHAPTER ONE

❧ ❧ ❧

I am tired and I want to sleep, but my mother nudges me forward. She is frightened now. I can feel her fear, but she does not try to run. I do not know where the danger lies.

For the first hour or two, I was brave.

I was.

I walked close to the foal and kept my chin high. I refused to look at any of my captors. My father would have been proud of me, I am sure. But then I began to worry, and I feel honor-bound to admit that I wanted to cry.

It had all happened so suddenly that it was hard for me to believe. My filly and I were prisoners?

We were.

And so was my aunt, Fallon.

The facts of the matter lay heavy on my heart. I am ashamed to say that I wasted a great deal of time feeling sorry for myself in the first few hours.

I know better.

I do.

It just all seemed like such a tide of misfortune—and none of it my own fault. Here I was, walking with the loveliest filly in all of Connaught beside me. She was not yet twenty days old, I was not yet ten years old, and both of us were captives. Here we were, walking tired and scared, following her muime—a placid, nursemaid milk cow.

The heifer had lost her own calf, then had saved my filly's life by letting her nurse. I was grateful to her.

My argument was with the man with the dark curly hair. The others called him Conall and looked to him for orders. He was in charge—that much was clear within moments of my capture.

Whoever they were, the boys and young men rode before and behind us—they had arranged themselves so I could not slip off into the woods.

Nor slow down.

Nor rest.

Nor even stop to allow the foal to nurse.

Conall had, at first, wanted the filly carried on some rider's mount. I had insisted on her walking, arguing with a shaky voice that having her slung over someone's saddle pad would scare her into fighting, and she might hurt herself.

He knew I was right. I could see it in his eyes.

I was, indeed. A grown horse's legs are fragile, and a foal's even more so—and even a small injury can lame a horse forever.

With a sharp lifting of his chin, Conall had agreed to have us walk. So now, with my filly's tiny hooves leaving little crescents in the soft ground, we went along behind the cows.

Don't mistake my meaning; I wasn't thinking about holding us back when I insisted. I realized afterward that the slower we went, the more easily my father would find us.

My aunt Fallon rode off to one side with her own guard—four of the young men rode in a tight formation around her. I found myself staring at her, I was so angry. They had put her on a calm, quiet horse. Her wrists were tight bound together, the reins held tightly by one of the young riders as he led her along.

The filly ticked a hoof on a rock, and I reached to steady her out of habit. She didn't need it. With every day that passed, she was more agile and stronger. Then I glared at Fallon again.

She is five years older than I am, and she is wild-tempered and mean. She is my father's sister, and all this was her fault, straight, true, and simple. If she had not thrown a rock and injured one of the boys, they would never have swarmed up the hill. The filly and I would never have been seen, much less captured. But Fallon was my father's sister, and they thought much alike.

What I mean is this: When either of them is angry enough—neither of them thinks at all.

The filly ticked a back hoof on something, and I tightened my hold on her halter. She was so tired she was clumsy. This was the time of morning when she would nurse, then nap in the sun. I hoped the boys would stop before too much longer to let her feed. I was afraid to ask yet; we had not been walking long, and I was not sure they would listen to me in any case.

There was one good thing: The red-haired boy who Fallon had hit with a rock seemed to be all right. He rode his horse steadily, not far from me. I could see him well. His eyes were bright and his chin held high. He was easy to pick out from the rest. His hair was as red as weathered iron, and there was a length of bloody linen tied around his forehead.

I saw him talking to his friends, laughing, and my heart was eased. From what I had managed to overhear from the boys riding close to me, he had not deserved such injury. The stone that had startled and infuriated Fallon had been small—and thrown soft and low—almost a joke. They all agreed that the one she had hurled back had been the size of a man's fist, thrown hard and with intent to harm. I had seen the same things; they were right.

As I was glaring at Fallon, the boys burst into loud laughter, and it startled the filly. She butted her slender muzzle into my side, and I put my arm around her withers to hold her steady. She was uneasy with all these strangers and had stayed very close to me all morning. I knew why. Bebinn was right—the filly thought I was her mother, and she expected me to protect her. I only hoped I could.

I looked again at my aunt Fallon. She was the cause of all our troubles—as indeed she had been the cause of many of the troubles in my life. But today, at least for now, she could not cause trouble at all, for anyone. She rode with her head lowered, staring at her bound hands.

I admit I took some small pleasure in seeing her like that at first. Fallon, who was always the bully, was being bullied for a change. Then I squinted and stared and realized that she was wriggling her wrists carefully, trying her bonds. Trust Fallon to find a way to make trouble, even when captured, bound, and guarded.

This will sound strange, but I didn't want her to break free. If she did, there would be a fight, and the men would chase her, the cattle would run, and my filly would shy and be terrified, and perhaps get away from me. She could so easily be trampled and hurt in a confusion of cows and horses galloping in all directions.

If Fallon got away, she would bring my father

and all the men of our tuath back to save me—but I could not imagine her getting away. There were twenty or more mounted boys and young men, and all would chase her. They had not put her on their best horse. They were not fools.

We seemed to be going northward. I wished we were headed west. My brothers were somewhere near the sea, fostered out and learning trades. I missed them, always, but now, captured and scared, I missed them even more. Trian and Fergal were growing into men—they had been so tall when last they had visited home. One day, one of them would come back to our tuath, to rule it as my father did now.

I spotted Conall, at the head of the riders. I had told him I was the daughter of the rí, that my father was king of our tuath. Knowing that did not seem to make him afraid to keep me prisoner.

I prayed to Saint Brigid for help, that my father would come soon to save us. Then I noticed that Fallon was still worrying her bonds, trying to break free. I tried to catch her eye, but she would not look at me.

I wanted to warn her off, to make her think. There was no need to take the risk of trying to escape on her own. I truly did expect my father and the men of our tuath to come galloping up behind us, thundering through the meadows before more than a day or two had passed. I was so sure of it that I didn't once think I needed to try to memorize the way we were going.

After all, I was telling myself, this much was certain: I could count on my friends to run for help. Bebinn and Gerroc were clever and brave. So were Dailfind and Inderb, and they were both older, taller, and longer-legged.

I knew that they would get some distance away from our high pastureland—where Fallon and I had been captured. Then Bebinn and Gerroc would drive the cattle while one or both of the older girls raced for help. Without the plodding cattle to slow the runners, they could make it home in a day or less. My father and his men, riding hard, would catch us up a few hours after that. My father would bring his hounds to track us. I listened for their baying, imagining them already racing toward us.

Oh, it was a wonderful tale I told myself, and it made me smile. The girls would run swift. Maybe there would be boys running the pigs in the forest who would see them, and they would take the news and run, fresh and even faster, the last stretch of the way.

Or, best of all, perhaps my father and his men had been—at the exact moment of our capture—only a small distance from our high pasture, coming to make sure we were safe and busy at our cheesemaking. That little bit of imagining lifted my heart. If that had happened, I would not be a captive much longer.

I smiled.

My father would be furious, I knew. And as soon as I thought it, I felt my smile fade. His daughter and sister had been taken prisoner, after all. This was beyond any man's capacity to bear. His men were all seasoned, experienced fighters. When they came galloping up behind us, swords drawn, shouting and fierce-eyed, they would scare most of these boys into a gallop for home.

Wherever that was.

I knew I would have to be careful to hear the hoofbeats before they got close so that I could pull the filly off to one side and hold her still and safe while Conall and the others rode hard to escape, scattering into the woods, leaving Fallon, me, the filly, and her cow-muime free to go home.

In my fanciful thoughts, I wove the tale an ending: No one would be hurt, my father would be glad to have the filly saved, and he would reward me by giving her to me, for my own.

Then, foolishly, I tried to imagine Fallon thanking my father and admitting it was all her fault. And that is where my daydreams folded up and collapsed. It was easier to imagine pigs growing wings.

Fallon would tell my father all this had been my fault, that I had distracted her from keeping watch. She would say the filly slowed us down when we tried to run. All of that was at least somewhat true, but sometimes she lied outright. She might even say that I had thrown the rock. Bebinn and the others had not seen anything, and my father would not likely believe me over his sister. He never had in the past. And even if he did, he would forgive her for throwing the rock because it was what he would have done.

Angry, I kicked at the ground and stubbed my toe. I heard one of the boys laugh as I limped a step or two. I didn't look up. I pretended I hadn't heard him.

The filly nosed at me, and I leaned to kiss her forehead. The boy laughed again, and I ignored him once more. Fallon was glancing around and noticed me looking at her. She scowled.

I looked away. Well, then, that much was settled. She was angry with me. If we ever were saved, she would tell my father whatever served her best to tell.

The filly pushed against me, and I stroked her neck as I walked, keeping my eyes on the rump of the milk cow who plodded along before me. Like most cows, she was so used to being driven that she simply kept at the pace of the animals and people around her without any herding at all. So long as there was no commotion, and she was allowed to graze now and then, she would walk to the end of the earth without balking.

I tried to stop thinking, except to listen for hoofbeats behind us. I rested one hand on the foal's back, lightly, and she sidled closer to me. I sang a low tune to calm her—and myself. She liked my singing, and lifted her muzzle to scent my face. Her breath was always milk-sweet, and I felt my heart lifting.

All my life I had wanted my own foal, my own horse. If my father would only give her to me, I would dance with joy.

When I glanced back at Fallon, she was preoccupied again, staring at the leather that tied her wrists together. It was clear enough. She would keep working at her bonds until she managed to get them off. If they left her alone long enough, she would probably *chew* through the leather.

She had a rare gift of making things worse.

I knew it would not be long before she caused more trouble of some kind. I could only beseech gentle Brigid and the rest of the saints and whoever else might listen to my prayers that my father would come soon.

CHAPTER TWO

The mornings are chilly, and I walk close to my mother until the sun warms us both. She is scared, I can tell, but I cannot tell what it is that scares her. Her own kind?

That first day, we did not stop until midafternoon. The filly nursed while the cow grazed. Once she was full, she sank to the ground beside her nursemaid cow. In an instant, her eyes closed. I rubbed the cow's ears. She was getting tamer.

"The foal is tired."

Conall's voice startled me, and I whirled to face the man who seemed to be the leader of these boys.

"Of course she is," I told him, forcing my voice to stay even. "She has been traveling for hours, and she is not even a month old yet."

"Tell me your name, please," he said. "And the other girl's."

I could not see what difference it made, so I told him. "I am Larach. Her name is Fallon."

He drew his lips into a thin smile. "Where did you find the gray mare, Larach?"

He had asked me that once before, just before he had made me his prisoner. I hadn't answered it then and I wouldn't now.

My eyes filled with tears, though, remembering how kind the mare had been, how I had run to the earthen-walled rath every morning to see if her foal had arrived. I was scared and tired. I turned away to wipe my eyes.

"Where did you find her?" Conall repeated.

I turned back to look up at him. "It was my father who found her. And he will explain it to you soon enough."

He frowned.

Then he walked away, calling for one of the boys.

I sat down beside the filly and laid my hand lightly on her shoulder. She did not move. She was sound asleep.

"Tsssst!"

It was a tiny sound and at first I thought it was some insect whirring its wings.

"Tsssssst!"

I looked around. Ah. It wasn't wings. It was Fallon, from the other side of the camp. She had been guided to a place in the shade of an old oak tree and sat now with her back against it, her hands still tied before her.

Her eyes were fierce, even at this distance. She made a little gesture, jutting her chin out. I looked in the direction she had indicated and saw Conall talking to a group of the young men.

Fallon tilted her head toward them, then brought her hands up to one ear. Well, that was clear enough. She wanted me to go listen, to see if I could overhear anything they were saying.

I was, I supposed, to somehow make myself invisible as I crept toward them across the open grass of the meadow.

I looked down at the filly. Even if there had been trees to hide behind, I would not have done it. I was not leaving the foal alone, not even for a moment. There were cattle grazing all around her. Any commotion at all and she might be trampled. The cow let her nurse, but she wouldn't protect her the way she would have protected her own baby. In that way, I *was* the filly's mother.

I shook my head, making it a small movement and gazing off in the distance while I did it in case any of them were watching.

"Tssssssst!"

I shook my head again without looking back at Fallon, and she went silent, seething in fury, I was sure. I saw the boy with the bandaged forehead walking toward me, and for a moment I thought he might hit me or take some other manner of revenge. I got up and moved to stand between him and the filly.

"I did not throw the rock, nor did the foal," I said in a low, even voice, trying to stand up straight enough to meet his eyes. He was taller than I by a good bit.

"Here," he said simply, extending his arm. He was holding a piece of dark bread.

Looking into his face, I saw that he was closer to my age than I had thought. His height had come suddenly, I could tell. Any boy's leine was shorter than what a girl would wear, but it was easy to see that he had grown a lot this past year. His belt had very little cloth gathered above it.

He blinked, and I realized I was staring. I blushed and took the bread from him. "Thank you."

He tilted his head toward Fallon. "Is she from your tuath?"

I nodded.

"Is she your friend?"

I shook my head. "She is my aunt. I am very sorry about your wound."

He gave me a nod of thanks for my sympathy. "I am not even the one who threw that last pebble. Is she always like that?"

The sweet smell of the bread was making my mouth water, and I took a bite before I answered. "Usually."

He shook his head. "What made her that way?"

I was stunned into silence. He didn't know Fallon at all and he was asking the question it had taken me most of my life to think about at all. "She seems to be better suited to men's work than women's," I said, wondering if he would understand me.

He nodded as though he did, then he looked past me at the filly. "She is a beauty."

I glanced at him. "She's overtired with all the walking."

He smiled. "What have you named her?"

I shook my head. "I haven't," I admitted. Then I closed my mouth, feeling awkward and embarrassed. This boy had somehow asked two questions that had caught me off gaurd.

I had thought it would not be my right to name the foal until my father said that she was mine. But with the turn things had taken, that would probably never happen. I felt the hair on the nape of my neck prickle. I could not stand the thought of her belonging to someone else.

The boy was watching my face. I must have looked confounded and worried all at once because he took pity on me.

"I'll help you think of a name," he said. "And I'll tell Conall that I have a headache long before sunset. He'll camp early, and your little foal can get some rest."

I was stunned by his kindness and struggled to think of something better to say than a simple thanks. I couldn't, so I managed to say thank you and then blushed again for no reason I could name.

He smiled once more, then turned and walked away, leaving me to wonder what kind of boy so easily forgave an injury that might have killed him or taken his sight. Perhaps, unlike my father or Fallon, he was not overeager to get even for each and every pain his life contained. I had to wonder now—what had made this boy that way?

As he walked away, I knew without looking over at her that Fallon was glaring at me. This would be one more thing that she would tell my father to make sure that he was angry with me—I had spoken kindly with an enemy.

I tore off a mouthful of the bread and positioned myself with my back toward Fallon while I ate. It didn't take long; I was famished, and it was not a big piece of bread. Once I had finished, I shooed flies away from the filly's ears for a moment or two—no more than that. Then Conall's shout interrupted my thoughts.

"Ready yourselves!" he called, his hands cupped on either side of his mouth. "We have far to go before we rest!"

I heard a few of the boys grumbling and wondered how long they had been traveling and where they lived. Their whispers faded when Conall strode past them on his way to mount his own horse. The cows were lifting their heads, their soft eyes watching the boys move to stand behind them. They knew that their time to graze was ending, and they wrapped their long tongues around one last mouthful of grass and tore it off as they lifted their heads.

I got up slowly. The filly sighed when I nudged her. She shook her spiky corn-silk mane as though I were a fly she could drive off.

I patted her neck and slid my hands down across her shoulders and sides. She lifted her head, her heavy lashes close together, her eyes half shut. Then she opened them, arched her front legs, untangled herself, and stood up.

I stood close to steady her. She was like a little child full of milk and dreams. She rubbed her muzzle on my leine, then tickled my chin with her breath. I scratched gently behind her ears, then down the center of her back.

With all the boys milling around, preoccupied, I reached inside my brat and felt the warmth of the little gold horse-shaped brooch I had found between the earthen walls of our rath. I was glad I had hidden it from Fallon—and everyone else. It was very old, of course, and it was precious to me.

I looked around again. The boys were still busy tightening belly-bands and checking bridle straps.

"Don't touch me, you swine!"

I looked up to see Fallon standing beside the horse she had ridden all day. However they had gotten her up there the first time, I don't know, but she was refusing to let them lift her back on her horse now.

The young man who had tried to help her up stepped forward again and she rounded on him. "I said get away!" she screeched.

I stood close to the filly.

This was what I had been dreading.

I tightened my grip on the filly's halter and put one arm around her neck. I could feel her trembling; her instincts were telling her to be ready to flee. Mine were telling me the same thing. I glanced at the edge of the forest. If the cattle began to panic, I would get the filly to the shelter of the trees.

I eased forward to grab the short lead that dangled from the milk cow's halter. I had to keep her with us. Without her, the filly would not live.

"You would rather walk?" Every eye in the camp swung from Fallon to Conall standing on the other side of the little clearing. His hands were on his hips.

Fallon lifted her chin another notch. "I would rather be released to go to my own home," she shouted. Her voice was shrill enough to sound like iron scraped on stone. She shifted her weight from one foot to the other and raised her bound hands. "You will be sorry," she announced angrily. "My brother will find us, and he and his men will make you sorry for harming me."

"Do we have *two* women of the royal house of mud and cow dung among us, then?" Conall asked in a voice that dripped with false politeness. "Their perfumed clothing and fair beauty should have informed us."

There was another round of uneasy laughter,

and I found myself understanding his anger and smiling at his joke. He was certainly right. Neither of us looked like royalty—his clothing was richer than ours by a good bit. He wore clothes like the young Normans who came to eat us out of house and home each spring. He rode a fine horse. All of the boys rode very good mounts. He was right. My father's tuath was not wealthy.

Fallon opened her mouth to shout and apparently could not think of anything vile enough to say, because she closed it again. For a moment, she looked like a fish. There was more laughter.

I hid my own smile by pretending to brush bread crumbs from my mouth. I wondered if Conall was rí of his tuath. From his fancy clothes and his well-bred horse, it was likely that my father's honor price was not nearly so high as his—the justicar always based fines on a man's wealth.

"Be still," Fallon cried out over the laughter. "All of you! In our tuath, we do not capture unguarded girls who are working to feed their families. How dare you—"

"Let her walk!" Conall called out suddenly,

interrupting Fallon's shouted accusation.

I watched the young men standing around Fallon back away from her slowly, without turning, the way one moves away from a snarling dog. One of them was talking to her, too quietly for me to overhear.

As Fallon stood, waiting for the men to mount their horses, she turned to look at me. I glanced away. I could feel her gaze piercing my skin, but I refused to look at her. I hoped the young men would keep her between them as they had done when she was riding. I did not want her to walk with me. I didn't want her that close to the filly when she started real trouble.

"Be careful," Conall shouted. "Keep her between you."

I exhaled in relief as the young men who had flanked Fallon's horse all day now moved to ride in the same formation again—before, behind, and on either side of her again, even though she was now afoot.

The filly shook herself. She rubbed her face along my shoulder. I let go of her halter, then reached for it again when she was finished scratching. She pretended to shy at my hand, swinging her head from side to side. She was no longer afraid. She wanted to play. I was glad she wasn't frightened now, but this was hardly a good time for games.

"Not now," I said in a low voice. "Just let me..." I took a step forward, but the filly leaped backward, rearing and spinning to gallop a short circle around me and the cow. She lifted her head and trilled a whinny, her voice still as high as a bird's whistle.

Another chorus of laughter broke out from the boys—they were watching me now. The filly shied at the sound and raced another circle, kicking up her heels this time. They all laughed louder.

Conall led off at an easy pace, and it suddenly struck me as odd that he hadn't pushed us all harder. How could he not worry that Fallon and I would have kin who would come after us? What rí had he ever met who would not ride after his captured daughter?

Conall's ambling pace made no sense.

Nothing did, I realized as I looked around the

clearing. Most of these boys weren't old enough to be cattle raiders, and cowherds were usually girls.

As the laughter died away, I could feel Fallon glaring at me, fury in her eyes—as though I had planned this to make light of her argument with Conall. The filly went around twice more before she danced around me, her hooves a light patter on the ground. She was so beautiful when she played, as though the earth had a lighter hold on her than it did on other creatures.

As we all began to walk forward, the boy with the bandaged brow caught my eye. "Daughter of the rí!" he shouted.

I looked up at him.

"Dannsair!" he called.

"Dannsair," I echoed, and the filly turned her head and met my eyes. Then she leaped to one side and spun to gallop around me. I blinked. She was a dancer.

It was the perfect name. I turned to smile at the boy and heard Fallon clear her throat, then spit in disgust.

I tell you true, I did not care.

CHAPTER THREE

It is strange how the land changes. We have passed through places where the ground is soft and oozes water and places that are more rock than soil. I want to gallop across it all, leaping over the rocks, but I do not. My mother could not keep up, and I am uneasy without her close.

Five weary days later we came to a river. It was deep and slow of current, and I did not want to cross it.

Fallon was still walking.

Of course.

She could not mount a horse with her hands bound and she would not suffer any of them to lift her up—indeed, they had given up trying, even the young man who sometimes talked to her as they traveled.

I had given up daydreaming and had taken up

worrying. Whatever had kept my father from coming after us would not be a small thing. I prayed he was well and that our tuath and my mother were all right. Bebinn and Gerroc would have told everyone what had happened, so at least my mother would know I was captured, but safe and well.

Dannsair and I were tired.

Dannsair. The name had attached itself to the filly as naturally as flowers are fastened to stems. I tried to catch the eye of the orange-haired boy now and then, but he seemed to have forgotten me entirely. It bothered me, but I knew it was probably best; my speaking to him again would surely send Fallon off into a shouting fit if she saw us. Fallon would already tell my father I had betrayed her, our tuath, the faeries, Saint Brigid, him, my mother, and God Himself by speaking once to an enemy. Heavens forbid I dare to do it twice.

When we stopped to wait for the boys to get the cattle across the river, the milk cow lowered her head and dozed. I rubbed her ears with one hand and held the filly's halter with the other.

I stood more or less patiently, but I was worrying

about how the filly would get across. More than once, I glanced back at the woods and could not stop my eyes from flooding with tears.

What could have had delayed my father and his men for so long? Would he ever find us? The herd of cattle had left a clear path of crushed grass and hoofprints, but many people shared these grazing lands and forests.

"Untie me!" Fallon shouted hoarsely—she had been doing a lot of shouting.

I don't think a single soul turned to look. I didn't. Conall seemed not to notice. I was very grateful for his quiet patience. If Fallon had been the captive of a less patient man, she would have been silenced long before this—with a rag tied across her mouth if need be.

I looked at the woods behind us, wishing I could chance an escape. I could find my way back, I was nearly certain. Dannsair nuzzled my shoulder, and I turned to feel her breath on my cheek. "Don't worry," I told her. "I won't leave you alone with them. I will never leave you alone."

She nibbled at my hair, and I raked it back with my fingers. I needed a comb and a bath and a clean leine. None of which I was likely to get, I knew.

Dannsair nudged me, then sprang backward and half reared.

"Not now, little one," I said quietly. "We can't play now." I reached to grab her halter and gently insisted that she stay close. We understood each other better with every moment that passed. She settled; then, after a moment, she positioned herself beside her muime, and the cow turned to nuzzle her as she nursed.

The cattle were milling and the herd boys were riding in circles, slapping their legs and making sharp little cries to make the cows move toward the river.

Letting out a long, uneasy breath, I stared at the water, scared for Dannsair. I could swim, but I had no idea if she could. I glanced at Conall, but his attention was on getting the herd of cattle bunched up and moving forward.

Cattle do not like to swim, but they can. The boys rode close on their heels, forcing them to wade into the water, then kept them moving until they were beyond wading. From that point on the they swam strongly toward the far bank on their own. I watched closely as more riders followed them in. The horses swam with their necks stretched out and their hooves thrashing.

The water was deep.

"Don't worry. The current is slow and lazy," I heard someone say behind me. I turned quickly. The orange-haired boy was riding forward, his eyes straight ahead as he guided his horse into the water.

The cows were on the far side, shaking water from their dark coats, moving off into the wide meadow beyond. They had come out of the river almost directly across from where they had gone into the water on this side. The boy had been right. Any current at all and they would have been pushed downstream.

Only I, Dannsair, the nurse cow, Fallon and her four guards, and Conall remained on this side of the river. Conall was occupied, talking to Fallon. He was right not to worry about guarding me. I could not escape without leaving both Dannsair and the milk cow behind, and he knew I would not do that.

Fallon and one of the young men were arguing.

He finally reached down, gripped her arm, and hauled her up by sheer strength. She beat at his back with her bound hands as his horse waded into the water, but she didn't try to slip off. Even Fallon is not foolish enough to think she can swim with her hands bound.

Conall was riding toward me. "Shall we go?" he called.

"I am afraid for the foal," I said as soon as he was close enough to hear.

He nodded. "As am I."

He dismounted and faced me. "My gelding is steady. Get up."

I stood between him and Dannsair. "I will not leave her."

Conall made a sound of exasperation. "Is everyone in your tuath so stubborn?"

I nodded.

"And so thickheaded?" he said, and I could see the corners of his mouth tug upward. "Get up," he repeated when I did not smile. "I'll put her across in front of me, and you can ride behind. It isn't a long swim and neither of you weighs more than a basket of apples."

"And the cow?"

He made the sound again. "She'll lead the way."

I pulled in a long breath, still nervous. But if there was a way out, I couldn't see it. Oh, how I wished Dannsair was old enough for me to ride. She would be swift as wind, and Conall's gelding would never catch us.

I locked my left hand in the gelding's mane and swung up. Conall motioned for me to scoot back until I was sitting nearly on the bay's tail.

Then Conall hoisted the filly up and over in one smooth motion. Before she could react, he had her over the gelding's back, on the thick saddle pad just behind his withers, her forelegs dangling down one side and her hind legs the other.

Then he mounted, nearly kicking me in the mouth with his right foot. I flinched and leaned backward at the last second. Once he was settled, I slid forward just far enough to be sure I would stay on. I kept my hands at my sides. I would not cling to his cloak like a frightened baby.

Through all of this, the gelding didn't move a hoof or twitch an ear. He stood still as rock until Conall leaned forward—then he responded instantly. Slapping at the nurse cow's rump with the ends of his reins, Conall started her toward the water.

I could hear Fallon arguing with her guard, and I prayed to Saint Brigid, that gentlest of saintly women, that my aunt would not start screaming and scare Dannsair. If the filly struggled and wrenched free...

I held my breath.

Conall guided his horse toward the water, driving the cow ahead of us. The cow waded in and swam without any fuss at all—she could see the herd on the far side and knew where she was to go. Dannsair flinched when the water hit her dangling legs, and I flinched an instant after. It was *cold*.

"There's the girl," I heard Conall say quietly. "It won't be but a moment and we'll be out."

I was touched by his concern, then realized he was talking to my filly. I leaned out just enough to see that he had draped the reins over the bay's neck and was using both hands to steady Dannsair.

I was grateful for his care, but I felt something

else, too, something deeper. I didn't want him touching her. On the far side of the river, Conall let me slide down, then he dismounted and lifted the filly to the ground. He was smiling and started to say something, but I ran up the bank, knowing Dannsair would be at my heels. I didn't stop until I had found the nurse cow, and then I did not look back.

It began to rain that evening. For the next few days we were wet and miserable awake and sleeping. Finally, the rain eased, then quit. The sun shone one morning, then winked out beneath clouds by noon. It did not rain again that day, but the sky stayed gray and thick.

I did not know where we were going and pride kept me from asking Conall. He was not a rí, I was coming to think. He did not act anything like my father. He spoke quietly to the boys and was unfailingly polite. He didn't give orders to anyone. He simply asked and they obeyed. I began to think he was the right hand of the rí—and that the rí himself must be very fierce to have his authority so respected even when he was not near.

Thinking this, I expected to come upon a

grand rath with many horses inside the circular earthen walls and so many cattle that twenty cowherds were needed. There would be well-tended barley and oat fields, corn already knee-high, and many houses. Or perhaps a Norman castle. That thought worried me. It was possible. I had overheard my father talking about Irish men who worked for the Norman barons.

I had seen Norman royalty—or their less important cousins and uncles anyway. They came to our tuath in the winter and spring, and they ate our food and drank our mead and slept on freshly made pallets in our homes.

We did not invite them. They were not our friends. We had to feed them and house them whenever they decided to travel or the Normans would make war on us. Every year, our tuath had to pay a portion of our grain, cheese, butter, and so on to my father, and he would take it to Athenry to give the Normans their share. He fought the Normans sometimes, but he wouldn't give them an excuse to come to the tuath with their swords at the ready.

Wherever we ended up, I wanted to see how

many fighting men they had. I wanted to know if my father could save us if he found us. If he could not, I would have to rely on myself to escape somehow, someday. Perhaps Fallon would calm herself enough to think clearly, and we could plan an escape together.

I had to believe it was possible. The idea of never again seeing my mother or Bebinn and Gerroc—and all the rest of my family—was too hard, too sharp; it scared me to my very bones.

One morning, coming up a valley into mounded hills, we saw a jumble of houses. They were crowded together, some of them so close their roof eaves were touching.

It was very odd.

There were no gardens, no fields planted to grain or peas. I saw Fallon staring as we came closer and wondered if she had known about such a place. My father must have known, though I had never heard him describe one.

There was no castle, no abbey being built, nor any river close by, so I knew it wasn't Athenry. I wasn't sure what an abbey or a castle would look like, but I knew from my father that they were both made of blocks of stone, stacked up like a fence wall, but much higher and wider. The only stone building I saw in this place was empty, its walls stained black. Had there been a fire?

This was someplace that mattered, though. I could tell that much. The wattle-and-daub buildings were lime-washed, neat and clean. And there were more of them—and bigger ones—than I had known existed in the world.

The boys veered off to drive the cows around the edge of the place. Conall gestured for the rest of us to go on. There were paths between the buildings, and we took the widest and straightest of these. I kept tight hold of Dannsair's halter as we went.

The nurse cow was just ahead of us as always. Buildings and swarms of men meant nothing to her. She clopped along at the pace of the horses as she had done through sunshine and rain, every day of her life. Dannsair was another matter. She pranced sideward, staring, her nostrils flared open.

I heard Fallon talking and glanced back to see her gesturing with her bound hands, arguing with one of the young men whose unhappy duty it was to guard her. She was *still* walking, of course, still refusing to be lifted onto a horse every morning.

Careful to keep Dannsair close, I peered into the doorways we passed. I saw a man working over a fire that burned unnaturally bright and hot inside one building. I saw three men hunched over a tabletop and wondered what they were doing until I spotted the piles of bones and antlers in a back corner; they were carvers.

Farther on, we passed linen-draped shades with people sitting beneath them with fresh-cut celeriac and cabbage laid out on wooden benches. Crowds surrounded them, and I saw a man offer a coin for a cloth sack of what looked like barley. I saw a woman selling carved bone combs, sewing needles, and belt catches. Had the men I'd seen carved them? The people were dark-skinned and light-skinned, tall, short, their hair a dozen colors. If this was a tuath, it was bigger than any I had ever heard about.

Conall kept us moving. The paths between the buildings were trampled completely bare. Not a blade of grass grew down the middles and there was no heather or lambs quarters—no plants of any kind, anywhere.

Nearly every building had someone at work in it. I glimpsed weavers and sword makers and a man making shoes unlike any I had ever seen my father wear. There were scents in the air I had never smelled before, some good and others vile. I heard someone singing a song I had never heard. I felt uneasy and excited and scared, all at once.

"This is Tuam," someone said very quietly. "It was mostly church abbey and graveyards in the long-ago times. Now crafters work here, and the tuatha and the Normans come to buy their wares."

I glanced up to see the boy with wild red hair riding near me. His eyes were fixed on the road ahead.

I looked forward, too.

"Do they all *live* here?" I asked, barely moving my lips.

"Most," he said. "Many are masters of their trades. Some have families here, others leave them at home, wherever they come from."

"Do you live here?" I whispered.

If he heard me, he didn't answer. Or maybe he

just didn't have time. An instant later, Conall's shout rang out.

"Cormac!" he shouted. "Ride on ahead and let them know we are coming!"

The boy leaned forward without looking at me, his horse lifting into a canter, then flattening out into a gallop.

Cormac. Well, now I knew his name at least. I watched him ride, perfectly balanced, his body moving with the horse's so that they looked like one creature. I imagined flying along on Dannsair's back one day, the wind in my hair, the ground blurring beneath her hooves.

CHAPTER FOUR

Walking in the rain is slow and hard. The mud sucks at my hooves, and the cold seeps into my body. At night, my mother lies close, and we try to keep each other warm.

Three long, cold, rainy days later, with the sun sinking low, we came to another odd place. There were buildings, but they were strange. Three were bigger than any house I had ever seen, wide and very long. Did the family of the rí live in them? What a big tuath this must be!

The whole place was set on a slope, the ground rising steadily. I could see four more big houses near the top of the hill, though they were not nearly so long as those below. Beyond all the paths and buildings, I could see stonework pasture walls, but from there the land dropped away, and I could not see far enough to tell whether they held horses or cattle or sheep or goats—or pea fields.

Two men noticed us coming and walked toward us down the hill, following a deep path worn by many hooves. Watching them come closer, I shivered. We were all damp through from the rain, and it was late in the afternoon and getting chilly—but I was also uneasy. This was a strange place.

I saw no sign of women working their gardens or bringing sheep or cows into folds for the night. I saw no goats or pigs—and no little children. There was no dairy byre that I could see. There were no walls of earth to enclose and protect stock and people—there was no rath.

I glanced around, hoping to see Cormac. Surely this was where Conall had sent him, to warn of our arrival. I had expected families, little children who would want to get a look at Fallon and me—and the filly. I could not see a soul besides men and boys, mostly those I had traveled with all these long weary days.

Conall held up one hand and everyone halted

except the cattle; they kept walking. "Get them to the east pasture," he called, and the boys veered off, both horses and cows walking slowly. The days of cold rain had stolen all our high spirits.

"Is the rí still here?" I heard Conall ask the men who were walking toward us.

"Yes," the taller one answered.

"Has he heard Cormac's tale?"

Both men nodded.

"Then take her to him," Conall said.

I jerked around, ready to argue, to insist that I needed to stay with the foal, but he wasn't talking about me. Of course. I was not the one who had thrown the rock. Now I understood why Cormac had been sent ahead. He had wanted to give the rí time to think about how to deal with Fallon.

"I will not go," Fallon said loudly.

Conall shook his head. "Oh, but you will. And I warn you, he hasn't got anything like my patience. His occupation doesn't require it."

Fallon lifted her head to snap an answer, but the guard she had argued with earlier said something quietly and she glared at him, then closed her mouth.

I stared at the guard. He was tall and broad and he had a pleasant face. He had not drawn his sword, he was not threatening her. He had only spoken, and he had done that quietly. I could scarcely believe it. Had he *reasoned* with her? How? I could not think of another time in the whole of my life that I had seen someone tell Fallon to hush, and she had. Not even my father.

The men on horses stayed in close formation around her as she was taken up the hill. She did not even glance at me as she passed. But whether she was still angry with me, or only worried about what the rí might do to punish her, I could not tell.

Conall turned to the boys and young men who remained. "Put your horses in. Rub them down well before you seek your own supper."

They all slid off their mounts and led them in various directions. I watched, puzzled. Put them *in*? Where was the rath?

When I saw the first young man lead his horse into one of the four long, thatch-roofed houses, I squinted, sure I was imagining it.

But I was not.

One by one they all led their horses *into* the

buildings. I could only stare wearily, my right hand on Dannsair's halter, my left on the cow's neck. These were not byres or pig houses, mind you. They were big. My mother would have been thrilled to live in any one of them. I shivered again. Thinking about my mother made me sad.

"Come with me, Larach," Conall said, dismounting.

Confused and stiff with fatigue and chill, I walked behind him toward the smallest of the huge buildings. My cold-numbed hand was on the foal's halter, but the truth was that Dannsair followed me now like any foal follows her mother. And the cow kept close to us both.

Conall pulled the door open and led his horse inside. As I went in behind him, I could only stare. The whole place was divided into small rooms, with walls that went only as high as a horse's back. I blinked, my eyes adjusting to the dim interior of the building.

"Here," Conall said, swinging a gate open on its leather hinges. "Use this one. In a month or two, this barn will be full of foaling mares. Until then, it will be all yours."

I looked up at him. He was pointing. "There are oats and corn in the boxes by the wall. I will have the boys bring you food."

I nodded.

"Take very good care of this filly and you will go home safe with the rí's thanks and a tale to tell," he added. And with that and not another single word, he walked away.

I was relieved to know that he understood how much the filly had bonded with me—that if I were taken away from her, she might grieve and refuse to nurse. What Conall didn't know was that I would take *very* good care of her—then I would, somehow, escape him and his men and take her home, where we both belonged.

I was surprised to see wheat stalks and pond rushes covering the dirt in the little enclosure. It was a deep, dry layer of bedding that would warm us all. I was grateful.

The cow balked. She had probably never been inside a byre in her life—this was her first year in milk. I had to get behind her and push while Dannsair stood shivering, her head down. When I finally had them both inside, I sat down and watched the filly nosing at the cow's udder. As she began to nurse, I lay back, intending to rest for a moment.

It was a big place, bigger than any house I had ever seen. I yawned, looking straight up. The roof was supported by massive timbers, and the thatch looked thick and tight. I could not hear a single drop of rain coming through. I shut my eyes.

That's where I woke the next morning, curled around Dannsair's back as always, my clothes finally dry all the way through. There was a trencher of oat bread and apples outside the gate. Someone had come to give me supper, had taken pity on me, and let me sleep.

CHAPTER FIVE

I can hear rain, but we are warm and dry. My mother and I play in the piles of dried grass. It is a good place. We slept soundly most of the day.

Dannsair and I were left alone that first morning and most mornings after that. Each evening, a boy brought me enough food to last until the next sunset. None of them would answer my questions about this place and who lived here. Conall had instructed them, I was sure.

I usually ate while Dannsair nursed, then I took her out of the little half-walled room to walk to the well. On days when it was raining hard, we stayed inside. She galloped and played in the wide aisle that ran the length of the horse-house. I knew Dannsair needed to rear, race, and buck if she was going to grow up strong and swift.

One morning, early, I went to the well to clean and fill the oaken bucket of water for Dannsair and the cow—and myself. I heard voices and looked up the hill to see Fallon and one of her guards walking between the houses. He was close at her side, not behind or before her. She saw me and raised her hand in greeting. I raised mine, wishing we could talk. Would she try to escape before the filly could leave the milk cow? Would she leave without me? I wasn't sure. But as little as I liked her, it was a comfort knowing I was not alone here in this strange place.

I fed the cow well. The stronger she was, the better her milk would be for Dannsair. The filly needed rich milk. She was growing fast.

When I took her out of the enclosure, I would run with an uneven stride, making my two-legged gait as much like a four-legged canter as I could. It delighted Dannsair, and she understood instantly; it was time to play. She galloped after me, rearing and kicking, her fluffy little tail flying out behind. We played every morning.

I was completely out of breath and laughing the morning that the wide door at the far end of the horse-house creaked open. I stopped in the middle of the aisle. The filly pivoted into an astoundingly tight turn, rearing to wrench around and gallop away from the intruders. She skidded to a stop before me, then dodged past and hid behind me.

It was Conall.

He was not alone.

His companion was a big, dark-bearded man who burst into laughter, slapping Conall on his shoulder. The filly started in fear, then stood closer. I felt her whiskers brush my elbow.

"Old friend, you are a marvel," the big man said. "I send you to trade horses for cows, and look what you bring back to me!" His smile faded into seriousness. "Conall, I am grateful."

Conall smiled, clearly pleased with the man's reaction. I stared. Was this the rí? Probably. I felt the filly's breath, quick and warm, against my back. I could feel her moving, and I knew when she peeked out from behind me because both men laughed. She shivered and pressed against my legs.

"You are scaring her," I told them. I tried to make my voice like my mother's when she is angry. Cold. Tight. Dignified.

"Are we now?" the stranger said. He was smiling the way a man smiles when a hound pup shows unusual intelligence. Had he not expected human speech from me?

"Yes," I said, both angry and scared. "You gave no warning coming in and startled her. I understand that I am a captive, but she does not."

Conall frowned at me. "Be respectful to the rí, Larach." Then he turned to face the big man. "As I told you, she chose to come with the filly, to be our guest."

The big man looked at me. "Conall is honest in all things."

"He is telling the truth now," I said. "But he is not telling all of it."

The rí looked puzzled, his brows hunching up in an exaggerated way. I stared at him, my heart thudding in my chest.

Then I took a deep breath and began talking, politely, respectfully. I told him the entire tale, starting with Conall coming so close to our herd that the cows nearly mixed, then coming back again and risking it a second time.

"We didn't know they were there at first, then one of the boys spotted the foal," Conall said evenly, interrupting me. "We went back to get a better look, and the other girl, Fallon, threw the rock."

"One of your boys threw the first stone," I said.

"What is your clan?" the rí asked me.

I hesitated. Would he try to get a judgment from the courts against my father? He might demand that my father pay him for the injury to Cormac. His honor price would be high. I could just imagine my father's anger if that happened.

Anger at me, I mean.

"Ah," the rí said after a moment. "Only the guilty of heart hide their names."

That did it. I am my father's daughter, after all. "And only the foolish put their fathers in the middle of an argument that has nothing at all to do with them," I said in a careful, polite voice.

"Oh, but it does," the rí said. "The gray mare was not his."

I frowned.

"Listen, girl," he said in a low voice. "That mare was brought shipboard from across the ocean, from the warm lands past the isle of Britain. She had a brand on her jaw—an intricate design."

He saw my face change.

I could not hide it.

"That gray mare was stolen from me. Her bloodlines were rare enough," he added, "and this foal was sired by one of the finest destrier stallions in all Connaught."

I cleared my throat. "My father found her running loose with a broken bridle," I said. "He did not steal her, but she was stolen from him by raiders. All our broodmares were stolen."

The rí turned to look at Conall.

He shook his head. "Not us. We rode to trade for the cattle, nothing more."

"My father *found* the gray mare," I repeated. "The raiders who stole her from us abandoned her when her labor began. I found her dying near our dairy byre on upland pasture. My father will be looking for us," I added, and watched their faces. Neither looked worried.

Conall turned to me. "Is your father a tall man with dark hair down his back who rides a heavy-boned bay?"

I looked at him.

He could read the answer on my face because he smiled. "I thought so. You look like him. So does Fallon."

He faced the rí again. "We saw him and his riders going east, riding hard, two days before we spotted the motherless foal among the cattle," Conall said. "I imagine he was looking for the raiders who stole his broodmares."

Dannsair nibbled the rim of my ear, and I covered it with one hand, thinking hard. Conall had seen my father riding east? No wonder Conall had been unafraid to travel slowly. My father had been riding away from us.

Dannsair stepped out from behind me, and I saw the rí's face light up looking at her.

"I agreed to come along to take care of my filly," I said, not weighting the word *my*, but not didn't skipping over it lightly, either. I could feel tears pressing against my throat and stinging at the corners of my eyes.

I pulled in a long breath and steadied myself. "She thinks I am her mother," I said. "She saw me first in this world, and she looks to me for protection."

I felt Dannsair nudge me just below my shoulder blade. I put one hand behind my back so she could nibble my fingers.

"The mare that birthed this foal belonged to the Baron of Athenry," the rí said slowly and loudly, as though I were both deaf and simple. "Her sire belongs to me. The filly is not yours."

I forced myself to look straight into his eyes. "I cared for that mare for most of a year," I said. "She was wounded and had nothing but skin stretched over her bones when my father found her. She would have died along with her foal."

"I thank you for your care," the rí said. He took a breath, meaning to add more, I think, but I kept on. I had to explain, had to make him understand.

"I saved this foal's life," I told him. "She had one foreleg bent under and would have died within her dying mother if not for me. The raiders ran the gray mare into exhaustion, and she could not..."

Then my trembling got worse and my voice just faded out and I could not make it come back. I missed the gray mare. She had been so kind to me. And I was so scared of losing the filly, too. I loved her.

"Come with me," the rí said abruptly. "I will show you the foal's father."

I shook my head and turned to put one arm around Dannsair's neck. "The filly won't let me leave her," I told the rí, my heart beating against my ribs. Maybe they meant to steal her from me here and now.

The rí was shaking his head. "You are more protective than her own mother would have been."

"No mare walks away from her forty days' foal," I said, just to say something. "If it couldn't follow, she wouldn't leave it."

I saw his expression change and he glanced at Conall, then back at me. "And how old would a foal be before a mare walked away?"

"Without looking back?" I asked.

He nodded.

I took a moment to think about it. I had

watched the mares in my tuath all of my life. Spring foals were usually weaned by Samhain, the mares bunching together in the pasture, their offspring forming a second group. "A hundred ninety days, at the youngest," I said. "Maybe a little older. And the colts would still follow if they could."

Once I said that, they both stared at me.

"It's a pity you're a girl," the rí said finally. "Bring the foal. We'll show the daughter to her father." I nodded. I really had no choice, and the truth was, I very much wanted to see Dannsair's sire.

As we walked, the rí told me that the gray mare had been brought on a ship from a land of sun and scented herbs. She had been sold first to a Norman in England, then was brought on to Dublin by ship, then overland, finally here, to Connemara. I believed every word of it. She had been graceful, and tall, and like no horse I had ever seen.

The stallion had been bred by someone to the west, he told me, a Connemara Irishman who had sold him for seven mares, two goats, and a curly-haired bull.

I will tell you true: He was worth every bit of that and more. When we came to the stone wall that held the stallion, I had to stop and stare. I'd never seen such a beautiful horse in all of my life.

He was a little taller than the gray mare had been, and he was heavier-bodied. The crest of his neck was as curved as a bow. They had named him Gealach, and it suited him perfectly. *Moon.* It described his color, the strange gray-white, silvery color that Dannsair had inherited. His mane and tail, like Dannsair's, were dark as midnight and floated like silk when he ran.

The next morning, I walked the filly up there myself, careful to keep to the edge of the woods, well away from the houses.

Gealach was racing the wind, galloping around the field. I caught my breath and stood watching for a long time. Only when he slowed to a trot, then halted, tossing his head, did I notice how they had enclosed him.

The little stone wall sat atop an earthen wall formed exactly as our rath's walls had been. Long ago, a deep ditch had been dug and all the earth from it thrown out to one side, then smoothed

CHAPTER SIX

My mother leads the way every sunny morning. I love to gallop. I can now jump the fallen log at the closest edge of the forest.

It was a long time before I talked to Fallon again—more than twenty days. I know this because one cloudy evening, alone in the big building, playing in the aisle with the filly, I stepped on a shard of bronze.

It was a broken knife tip from one of the rush cutters' scythes—or so I thought. It was no longer than my little finger, and the edge was dulled, or it would have cut my foot.

I gouged a little mark in one of the wood posts that formed the filly's enclosure at sunset and added another one each day thereafter.

I got tired of being alone. One morning, the filly and I started up the path toward the houses where people seemed to live. Before I could reach them, a man stopped me.

Politely, without raising his voice, he told me not to come any closer. "You are not allowed up there," he said.

I asked him why. I asked him who had given him his orders.

He did not answer either question.

I was about to turn and walk back to the meadow below when I caught a glimpse of movement over his left shoulder. It was Fallon, farther up the hill, walking alone. She made an arcing gesture with one hand, drawing a half circle in the air.

I understood instantly and turned to walk back down the hill. But this time, I went past the barns and into the meadow below, the filly trotting to keep up.

I cut across, following the invisible map Fallon had drawn in the air, heading in a long circle toward the woods. Once we were in the cover of the tall trees, I stopped to listen.

After a moment I heard Fallon whistle softly. I whistled back and headed toward the sound. We finally met in a dense stand of oaks. She embraced me for a second, which, as you may imagine, nearly took my breath away. Fallon was lonely, too.

"Are you being treated well?" she asked as she stepped back.

I nodded. "Well enough. But no one will talk to me."

She exhaled a long breath. "Only Brian speaks to me, a little. He is not supposed to." She almost whispered the last sentence. Her voice was different than I had ever heard it, and she had an odd look in her eyes. I had seen it before, in Bebinn's eyes when she talked about Tally.

It was clear as rainwater to me as she spoke: Fallon liked Brian. Enemy or not, she was drawn to him.

"We will escape as soon as the filly is weaned," I said, watching her face harden.

"That's months away."

I nodded. "I know, but I can't leave her."

Fallon shrugged. "You could just leave the

cow, too, so she won't starve. Conall will raise her. He knows more about horses than any man alive, I think. That's what this place is."

I shook my head. "What? What is it?"

"He raises horses," she said. "There must be fifty broodmares in the fields on the other side of the hill, all about to foal."

"This isn't a tuath?" I asked, wanting to make sure.

She shook her head. "All the boys are fostered here to learn from Conall. The young men come to learn, too, and the poorer ones work for a year in trade for a good colt. All the tuatha want better horses—faster and heavier—so they can win at war."

I reached out and put my arm around Dannsair's neck and drew her close. "They get horses to take back to their tuatha?"

Fallon nodded. "Brian's father is the rí of a tuath not far from here. He owns Dannsair's sire. I have not spoken to him yet." I had, of course, but I was not about to admit that to Fallon. She looked over her shoulder. "I have to go or Brian will be blamed for losing track of me."

I knew without asking which of the young men was Brian. He was the one who had talked to her as we were traveling, I was sure. She touched my arm again and turned to go. I hated to part from her so quickly. Who would ever have thought I would be eager to spend time with my aunt? Once we were home, would she be as mean to me as she had been before all this had happened?

I walked back through the woods, one arm over Dannsair's neck, thinking about every word Fallon had said, turning each one over and over like a crow does a shiny stone.

What Fallon had said fit perfectly with what the rí had told me. They were interested in breeding special horses here, horses with rare blood, fine horses that most tuatha did not have—that Norman royalty did not have.

I tried to imagine a life learning to care for horses. The rí had said it was a pity I wasn't a boy. He was right. It would be my happiest day, to be fostered out to a place that raised horses. But not for war…

I remembered, all too clearly, the gray mare's terrible wound when my father had found her.

Getting back to the meadow, I pretended to be leading Dannsair in a wide circle for exercise while I thought. I was so busy wishing I were a boy, that I could foster out here or somewhere else that raised horses, that it was a long time before I realized that Fallon had not pressed me about escaping. Maybe she had her own reasons for wanting to stay.

After my talk with Fallon, the days began to blur for me. All my life, I had been surrounded by relatives, by my whole tuath. I was still homesick enough to cry at night. But somehow, having spoken with Fallon, I felt a little better, a little less alone.

I wandered anywhere I wanted during daylight hours, Dannsair at my side. Conall wasn't worried about me escaping. He knew I would not leave the filly and that the filly could not leave the cow and live. Even if we started off at night and no one missed us until morning—we still wouldn't get far enough to give a horse more than a good gallop before we were caught again.

Each day a boy brought food, and there were others who ran here and there, doing chores. As

Dannsair grew and we spent more and more time outside the building, I saw the boys less often.

It hardly mattered. None of them talked to me. None of them even really *looked* at me.

Conall started coming to the barn every few days to look at the filly, to ask if she was eating well. Then he left. He said little else, but still, I looked forward to him coming.

The filly and I spent every waking moment together. I found myself talking to her as though she were Bebinn or some other friend. She was always attentive, tilting her head as though she was trying to puzzle out what I was saying to her.

Her halter became too small, and I thought about asking Conall for cloth to braid to make another one. But she followed me so closely on her own that I didn't ask. We truly had no further need for a halter.

Dannsair and I made friends of the cats that ate the mice that rustled through the bedding in the barn. It wasn't a bit hard, wild as they were. The cow gave more milk than Dannsair needed or wanted. I began milking her lightly in the evenings and leaving what I didn't want in a small pail.

The cats found it and began coming to watch me milk, hoping for supper. Dannsair was fascinated with them, and they learned to tolerate her sniffing and nuzzling in order to get their share of the milk.

We got to know two of the hounds that sometimes came around looking for rats for supper, too. I would close them in, sometimes, when we left to go walking. When we got back, they would be sleeping, full and happy—and the rustling of rats in the straw and rushes at night would lessen for a time.

It was like being at home in many ways.

I worked.

Every morning, I cleaned the soiled rush bedding out, piling it in the offal heap out in the meadow where the boys brought manure and dirty straw from the other horse-houses. By watching the boys, I learned that there was a huge stack of clean dried rushes mixed with wheat and barley straw sheltered beneath the timbered eaves at the back of each of the buildings. I carried in armloads until our little enclosure was clean and comfortable again.

Every day I filled the water bucket, then went back out to wash my face and hands at the well. After the filly nursed and the cow had been fed, Dannsair and I went outside.

The summer days were mostly warm and bright. Our walks got longer and longer. Sometimes, I took the nurse cow along, letting her graze in the meadows while the filly ran free, galloping in long loops for the sheer joy of it. The cow was so used to traveling with us that she stayed close without any effort from me.

When I led the filly down into the woods, no one followed me. If I needed more assurance, that provided it. Conall wasn't a bit worried about me running off. He knew I would never endanger Dannsair.

One fine day, I found a wooded creek and bathed. A few days later I returned and washed my leine, then wrung it out and put it back on to dry. I hid the gold pin high in a tree, then washed my brat and the piece of yellow cloth I had dried the filly with after her birth. I hung the dripping lengths of cloth in the same tree and came back for both the following day.

It felt wonderful to be clean and I went regularly to the creek. The cow and Dannsair always watched me bathe, the filly tilting her head. One day, she waded in the shallow water while I washed. She pawed at the water and finally lowered herself into the shallows to roll side to side. Her coat dried silky and clean in the sunshine.

Taking even longer walks as the filly grew stronger, I found two fields of grass to be cut later for winter feed for the stock and one of tall standing corn—which told me that summer was half over.

Dannsair and I often went to stand and watch her sire as he grazed alone in his walled field. I had never seen wild horses, but I had heard men talk about them, and I had listened closely. I knew that no free horse lived alone by choice—they stayed with their herds or found new companions and formed new bonds.

I wondered if Gealach was as lonely as I was. One day he whinnied, low and loud, staring at Dannsair, then he whirled and galloped in wild circles across the field. It was that day I saw Fallon again, from a distance.

She was walking with one of her guards. I couldn't tell, but it looked like Brian. She did not see me—she was turned toward him as they walked back over the top of the hill.

The next morning, a broodmare was led into the building by a boy I recognized from the long journey to this place, though of course I did not know his name.

He ducked his head by way of greeting and put the mare in one of the enclosures nearest the door. "The stalls will all be full before long."

"Stalls," I echoed, startled that he had spoken to me at all, but glad that I at least had a word for these little horse rooms. There were a dozen questions I wanted to ask, and I tried to sift through them to ask the most important one first. Before I could speak, he turned and was gone.

I walked to the stall and opened it so Dannsair could nurse. While I waited for her to finish, I counted the gouges I had made in the wood. Then I rocked back on my heels, amazed.

We had been in this place ninety-nine days. Had I counted right? Did these people not celebrate the bread feast of Lugnasad? I sighed then, realizing there were few women here, if any. It was my mother and her friends who remembered the old ways, prepared the bread, and led the thanks for early harvest.

And my father had not come? Maybe he never would. That thought lay like a weight on my shoulders. I ached with loneliness, then felt so angry I wanted to scream. It was wrong to want to talk to enemies. I had been taught that all of my life. My father would be furious if he knew I didn't hate Conall, that I wanted him to talk to me more often. If he knew that, he would certainly take the filly away from me even if I managed to bring her home. Just thinking that made my heart ache and my feet feel unconnected to the good brown earth. And it made me wish again that I was a boy.

My father was proud of my brothers. They came home each year for Samhain; each year they were taller and stronger and brown-skinned from fishing on the sea. The year before, Fergal's hair had darkened a great deal and Trian laughed less than I remembered. But they both said they liked the families who had taken them in.

I knew that the idea behind fostering was to make closer allies of the tuatha involved—to mend old feuds or to begin new friendships. If I were a boy, I might have been fostered here.

People thought my father had sent Trian and Fergal off to keep them safe from the endless warring. Perhaps it was true. My mother was glad they were far from the fighting. It made sense to keep them safe. My father wanted one of them as his heir, someone to become rí when he was old.

He had no such use for me.

I wondered for a long, cold moment if he would even bother to come looking for me. Then I remembered Fallon. He would want to find his sister, I was sure. They argued and he hated her shrill voice, but they understood each other. They were heart-bound.

Carrying my heavy thoughts, I walked to the bay mare's stall. The boy had given her oats and dried corn. She was calm and friendly. She was young. Her teeth were white and straight and her eye hollows were not deep. She looked like she might be rising four, no older than that.

While Dannsair cantered in circles in the aisle,

I climbed into the stall and scratched the mare's cheek and ears for a time, then gently ran my hands over her side. Her flanks were rounded. Her milk was coming in, too, I could tell. She would have her baby very soon.

Odd thoughts stabbed at my heart. By the time I saw my brothers again, would they know me? Would the same thing happen with my mother? Would I be gone so long that Bebinn and Gerroc and my little cousin Magnus wouldn't know me? That night, instead of sleeping, I cried.

CHAPTER SEVEN

I hear many horses. Their voices are not so far away. My mother does not often seek them out. We are a small herd, just ourselves.

Five days later, the filly and I rose early and she nursed, then stood by the stall gate looking expectant. I let her out into the long aisle, and she reared and kicked, then galloped a few strides before sliding to a halt. The bay mare put her head over her own gate and watched, her ears pricked forward and her eyes bright.

I went to pat her. She smelled my hands, then my cheek. I stood very still, the filly right behind me. I could see that the mare's udder was waxy looking and full. Her breath had a faint salt-sweet smell, too. Her foal would be coming *very* soon now.

"All is well?"

Conall's voice startled me breathless; I was so used to silence. Dannsair slid to a halt and whirled to face him, then galloped to hide behind me. She was so tall that she could look over my shoulder at him now.

"Yes," I managed. I wondered how long he had been standing in the doorway, watching me.

"Enough to eat?"

I nodded again.

"Both of you?"

I nodded once more. "The cow gives more than Dannsair and I need. Sometimes I feed the cats."

He smiled. "I am having three more mares brought in tomorrow," he said. "If you think the filly will be too disturbed, we can move you to a quieter place."

I looked at him. He did not care whether or not I could sleep through mares giving birth and boys coming in and out to keep an eye on them. He cared about Dannsair getting her rest. The truth was this: The last thing I wanted was more quiet.

"I would rather be here," I said. "I can help."

He shook his head. "No need. The boys will come get me if any mare has trouble."

He looked past me at the bay mare, then went into her stall. He rubbed her forehead, and then ran his hands down her sides as I had. "Three or four more days," he said.

"Sooner," I told him. "She is standing up to sleep every night now."

He shook his head. "That is an old idea."

I nodded. "My grandmother taught my mother, who taught me."

He looked at me and his face became very serious. "All horses stand up to sleep sometimes. Some do it more than others. It has nothing to do with the timing of a birth."

"She will birth tonight or tomorrow night."

He shook his head. "You are as stubborn as Fallon in your own way."

I bit at my lower lip. "Perhaps. But the foal is coming nonetheless. Smell the mare's breath."

He shook his head. "Her breath? That is another old woman's tale, I am sure. If there were a way to tell, I would get a lot more sleep this time of year. The other barns are filling up, too."

He came out of the stall and looked at me. He was silent just long enough for me to begin to feel uneasy. "It will soon be time for me to begin handling the filly some of the time," he said. "I want her calm with me before..." He glanced at the door, then back at me. "Before she is weaned."

I felt my skin prickle at the odd pause in what he had said. Of course. Once she was weaned, he would want to send me home.

"I will teach her what she needs to know," I said.

"Larach," he said. "She is not yours to train."

I lifted my chin and looked at him. If I could have pierced holes in him with my glance, I would have.

"I told you," I said very politely. "My father found the gray mare and I nursed her to health. And Dannsair would not have lived through her birthing if it weren't for me."

"Dannsair?" he echoed.

I frowned. "That's her name."

He smiled slightly. "I see. I remember the tale you wove about helping with the birth."

"It's not a tale. It's true."

He smiled again, with the same endless patience he had given Fallon's temper. "We think it more likely that mare and foal both survived a normal birth, then the mare died because you didn't know how to care for her and—"

"She died because the raiders drove her into exhaustion," I interrupted. "I told you. She was almost gone when I found her. The foal was in the wrong position and—"

"Enough," he said, interrupting. It was clear as daylight that he didn't believe me.

"It is the truth," I said, knowing I should simply be silent. "She was brave and she tried hard to live, but she just couldn't." I think it was hard for me to stop talking because it had been so long since I had spoken more than a few words to anyone. "The foal was so slow in coming that I was afraid and—"

He held up one hand to hush me a second time. "However it happened, she is here now," he said. "She is back where she belongs. When she is weaned, I will have you and Fallon returned to the dairy byre where we found you, and you can make your way home."

"You will never keep Fallon here that long," I said, just to have something to say.

He laughed quietly, shaking his head. "I won't have to try."

I wanted to say that I knew what he meant, that she was drawn to her guard, that she liked him and that I, too, knew his name, but I couldn't. If I did, he would know that Fallon and I had spoken.

"Please, Larach," he said quietly. "I know your father is always at war, always taking captives and fighting and..." He trailed off and exhaled slowly, closing his eyes. "The whole of Eire wars far too much," he said quietly.

I felt off-balance, as though the ground had shifted beneath my feet. I wanted to be angry with him, but he had voiced exactly what I had thought ever since I was old enough to think anything at all. There was too much war. Too many fights. I wanted to ask why he bred warhorses—but I couldn't, for the same reason I could not admit that I knew about Fallon and Brian. So I said nothing at all.

He turned to go and was almost at the door

when my lips pried themselves apart and I said something entirely foolish.

"I love Dannsair."

He turned back to look at me. "I know you do."

His eyes were sad, and I could not stop myself from pleading. "Then you have to understand. You can't take her away from me."

"I would not," he said. "But it will not be my decision. The filly is not mine."

I started to argue, but he shook his head. "The day the rí is sure the filly will thrive without you, he will want you gone. He has no wish to start a fight with your father."

"I will not leave her here," I told him.

He sighed. "If you were a boy, we could foster you with the rest. Or you could go to Athenry."

"Where is the rí's tuath?" I asked him, wondering when he would stop talking and lock me back into silence. "Why is he here most of the time?"

"It is nothing you need to understand," he said, his voice tightening.

"I know why you brought me," I said, speaking as quietly as he had. "You were afraid the filly would grieve and die without me. But Fallon? Why did you bring her?"

He exhaled. "Two reasons. The boy she hurt is the son of the rí; I thought he would want to deal with her. And I hoped that she would look after you and travel with you when it was time for you to leave."

I nodded, believing him. It made sense.

He was not unkind.

No matter how much I wanted to hate him, I could not.

"I had no idea how difficult Fallon would be," he added. "Or how much young Brian would like her. There are *two* rí who will not be pleased about that, your father and his."

The wry tone of his voice made me smile. Then, suddenly, I understood what he had said. Cormac and Brian were both sons of the rí who owned Dannsair's sire. The two boys were brothers. And Conall was right, my father would not like her choice of a young man.

Conall straightened his shoulders. "You must get used to the idea of losing Dannsair."

That made my heart fall and my eyes sting. I

had loved Dannsair since the night of her birth. Now, after all this time with her, I only loved her more. And if I left her here, she would end up in battle, sooner or later. She might be killed.

But I met his eyes and nodded. "I will try," I told him. And I could only hope that he could not tell that I was lying.

CHAPTER EIGHT

If I wake at night, my mother is already awake.
She touches my face or rubs my neck
until I fall asleep again.

I know better than to lay awake worrying. I do.

Worrying does no good.

But that evening, after I marked the day on the stall rail with my little piece of bronze, I lay awake. I could not sleep for thinking. If my father had not found us by the time Dannsair was weaned and no longer needed me—or any other mother—what would I do?

She would not be nearly old enough to ride by then. There would be no question of simply outrunning Conall and the others to escape until she was two or three years old. And the rí would not let me stay that long.

I turned over and forced myself to think about other things for a time, then gave up and lay on my back again. The rí might very well be willing to go raiding to recover a foal of rare blood. Maybe he would be enraged that I had eaten his food and been his guest, then stolen a filly he thought was his. I knew my father would react that way in the same situation. Would he fight the rí to protect me and Dannsair? I wasn't sure.

For a split second, I imagined angry raiders coming into the tuath because of me—and I remembered what my mother had said to me after Bebinn had been captured.

She had chided me to count my blessings. Raids were less common than when she was a girl, she had said. And the raiders had not found our main herd, they had not stolen chickens, pigs, or raided our gardens. They had not burned our houses. They had not killed anyone.

But maybe next time we would not be so lucky. An image of our houses in flames, our crops ruined, and our storehouses emptied came into my mind, followed quickly by others: old Orlaith shivering and starving; Bebinn sick and weak; my poor mother crying. Magnus, my beloved little cousin who could not run because of his limp, hurt because he could not get away.

These were not fancies beyond reason, I tell you true.

Wars in Eire had been fought for lesser causes.

And all this might come to pass because I had led an angry rí and his men back to my people. I could not do it.

My father would never forgive me.

I would never forgive myself. The truth was simple and painful: If I wanted to keep Dannsair, I could not go home.

But then, where would I go?

Dannsair lifted her head, then sighed and shifted, stretching out in the rushes. A few feet away, the cow stirred, then fell back into her slow, even breathing. I sat up, ready to touch Dannsair, to move closer to her so that she wouldn't waken.

It was in that instant that I heard the bay mare shake herself and begin to pace. I waited until

Dannsair had settled back into sleep, then I lay back down. I could see the timbers that supported the thatched roof. I had worried most of the night away—morning was not far off.

I heard the bay mare circling her stall, and I might have fallen asleep to the sound of her muffled hoofbeats, but then she groaned. It was a soft, low sound.

Knowing it was better to leave her alone unless she needed me, I got up and walked closer, but didn't go too near. I sat with my back against the wooden rails across the aisle from her stall.

In the murky predawn light, I watched the mare stand still, sometimes turning her head to look down the length of her own body as though she was wondering what was happening to her.

I hoped that nothing would go wrong. If it did, and I could not manage, I would run for help. Some guard would stop me, I had no doubt, but surely he would find Conall if I explained.

I dozed again, sitting there in the near dark. When I opened my eyes, it was light enough to see. The mare was lying down and her foal was beside her.

"You didn't need anyone interfering, did you?" I asked her gently.

She startled slightly. I had been so still she hadn't known I was there. I stood slowly and moved just close enough to see better. The foal was still wet with the waters that had eased its passage into this world. It was shivering. The mare was tired. She was young. This was her first foal, and she didn't know enough to lick her baby dry.

"I can help you if you will let me," I said softly. The mare looked at me. "Your foal needs to stay warm."

I went back to the stall where Dannsair slept. I lifted the old yellow brat from the rails where I had hung it after I'd washed it in the creek. It had dried Dannsair well enough, and it would work for this foal, too.

The bay mare held perfectly still when I came into the stall. Even so, I moved very slowly, asking her permission to touch her baby. She lowered her head to smell my hair and my face, then closed her eyes to doze.

I set to work.

The soft old brat dried the foal fairly quickly.

It was a truly handsome colt with long legs and a wide forehead marked with a slender curve of white. After a time, he stood up to nurse. I went to get his mother oats and a little corn.

I stood aside when I was finished, my back against the stall gate. Then I glanced down at her water pail. The mare's pacing had kicked up dust and chaff from the straw and rushes, and they floated in a scummy layer on top.

I lifted the pail and went out, sliding the wooden latch shut behind me. Outside, I peered up at the sky as I walked to the well. It was cool out and the air smelled like rain.

The mare drank eagerly when I set the bucket down inside her stall. She was so calm and content that I decided to take out the birth-soiled rushes and bring her clean bedding. Working slowly, one hand sliding down the mare's side to let her know where I was and what I was doing, I gathered up the dirty bedding and carried it out. Then I brought clean rushes in.

I found myself singing softly, an old song that my mother had often sung. I sighed when I realized that I had been captured and forced away from my home, all to end up doing what I had always wanted to do and could never do at home.

I was working with horses.

"Larach?"

It was not Conall's voice outside the door. It was a boy's voice, barely above a whisper. I recognized it instantly.

"Cormac?" I whispered.

"Yes," he answered. "Conall said to check on the mare and not to talk to you. But I heard you singing and..."

"The mare is fine," I told him, and smiled. "Come and look for yourself."

He opened the door and came in, leaving it standing open for the light. He peered into the stall.

"She needed nothing from me. She did a fine job," I told him. "I helped dry him a bit was all."

Cormac turned to grin at me, then looked back at the foal. "Him? It's a colt, then?"

"Yes," I said. "A beautiful little stallion."

"My father will be pleased," he said. "He wanted a colt. The mare belongs to the Baron of Athenry, but he's agreed to trade this foal for an older filly." He hesitated, then glanced at me. "I wish we could talk more."

I caught my breath. "Why can't we?"

He looked me in the eye and spoke quickly. "It's all more than you think. My father knows yours and they hate each other. Your father almost certainly did steal the gray mare after their last battle, and the Baron of Athenry—"

He stopped because we both heard footsteps at the same time.

"Run!" He gestured toward the stall where Dannsair slept. "Pretend to be asleep."

I hesitated an instant because I had been ready to defend my father's honor—I did not believe he would steal unless someone had stolen from him.

Cormac gestured. "Please, Lara. Run! He will send me home for talking to you."

"Cormac?" It was the rí's deep voice, and it unlocked my knees. I ran up the barn aisle, my bare feet nearly silent on the soft dirt. I leaped over the planks and sank, trembling, onto the rushes.

"Yes, Father?" I heard Cormac answer.

I lay down beside Dannsair and tried to still

the sound of my ragged breathing. She stirred at my touch, but did not waken. Only then did I remember that I had left the yellow brat hanging over the rails of the mare's stall.

"Filly or colt?" I heard Cormac's father ask quietly as he came in.

"Colt," Cormac answered him.

"What's that?" Cormac's father wanted to know.

I counted to seven before Cormac answered.

"Just a rag I found. To dry the colt."

"Well done," his father said. "Chill is hard on new foals."

I could hear the mare nosing the bottom of her feed bucket.

"I gave her a little corn," Cormac said awkwardly.

I lay still as a stone through all this. What choice did I have? I could hear the tenseness in Cormac's voice. It was astounding that his father didn't. When they left and I heard the door close, I waited long enough to be safe, then got to my feet.

My movement awakened Dannsair. She heaved

herself up onto her long legs and walked beside me out into the half-light that comes just before dawn.

"Cormac's father is my father's enemy," I told the filly. She stood close to me. I could feel the warmth of her coat through my leine, and I was grateful not to be alone.

My father's enemies—and all their kin—were my own enemies.

So I had been taught all my life.

If it was true, Cormac could not be my friend. Brian and Fallon were doomed to swear hatred for each other.

I watched the sun rise that morning feeling lost. Nothing made sense to me anymore. I wanted, more than anything, to talk to Cormac. A trade, he had said. An older filly for the new colt. What filly? Dannsair?

CHAPTER NINE

There are new foals. Their mothers keep an eye on me when I come too near. I am careful not to make the mares angry. I have no wish to be nipped. The foals love to gallop, clumsy though they are. It is a joy to play!

There were twelve more foals in the next twenty days. It was lovely, all those soft-eyed baby horses. I saw seven of them come into the world. For the other five, Conall or one of the other boys happened to come at the right time and stayed to watch, to make sure the mares had no trouble.

None did. I brought water once or twice. I kept the yellow brat clean and ready, and I dried a few of the foals because their mothers were young and exhausted. But I always listened carefully for footsteps and voices as dawn came nigh, and I ran for my stall the instant I heard anything. While Conall or one of his boys was there, I pretended to sleep.

Cormac did not come again. Nor his father. I wondered if they had left, gone back to their tuath, wherever it was. I had to wonder this, too: Had Cormac's father questioned him later? Had he admitted that I was the one who had dried the foal, that we had talked? Had his father gotten angry and made him leave?

As the days passed, more mares had their foals and were moved to the pasture once the babies were well up on their legs and strong enough to follow. And then there came a day when the barn was empty again—except for Dannsair, the nurse cow, and me.

In the daytime, Dannsair and I walked free as before, with no one interfering with where we went or when we came back so long as I stayed away from the houses on the hill. As he had all along, Conall knew I wouldn't try to escape, not until the filly was weaned anyway. And even then,

I would be foolish to try. Every time I saw him, I tried to look sad and accepting, as though I knew that once she was eating grass and had reached the age when her natural mother would have let her go, I would have to go home peacefully without making trouble.

Don't think I didn't try to invent some way around it. Don't imagine that I wasn't frantically thinking of ways to escape.

No matter how many times I thought it through, the facts did not change. If I took the filly away from her nurse cow now, while no one was watching us, she might starve before I found another foster mother to let her nurse—if I ever did.

If I took the heifer with us, we would have to go so slowly that we would be easily found before we got very far. And beyond all those worries, I had no idea where to go. I could not go home without risking hurting everyone I loved.

And there was something else.

I liked it there.

That may sound strange, but it is true as sunlight. I loved sleeping in the long barn. I loved the foals and taking care of the mares—even if no one knew I was the one doing it.

I fell into a new pattern as Dannsair began to nurse less often. We would bring the milk cow with us for the morning, then take her back to the barn so that I could let Dannsair play with the foals in the meadow.

There were always two boys watching the mares, sometimes three, but I stayed away from them and they did not bother me. I was sure they had told Conall that Dannsair was playing with the foals. Since he did not object, I could only think that he did not mind. I *loved* watching Dannsair leap and rear. She was the oldest and the biggest, but she was careful not to hurt the younger ones. They chased her in groups of five or six sometimes, and she would gallop just fast enough to keep the lead for a while. Then, sometimes, she would lower her head and stretch out her neck, bursting into her long natural stride and leaving them all far behind.

Fallon and I met in the woods again one morning. Brian had agreed to let her come talk to me, she said, so they had stood in sight on the path until she had been able to get my attention by waving and making the circular motion with her hand.

We made our way into the woods from opposite sides again, and this time, she was as frantic as I, but for a different reason. It was not her escape she was worried about.

"I want to marry Brian," she told me. "But his father will never allow it. I am not supposed to be talking to him at all—or to anyone else for that matter."

I nodded. "It's the same with me. They have all been forbidden." I said nothing about Cormac. Fallon was not good at keeping secrets, and I didn't want to cause Cormac trouble with his father. I knew, firsthand, what it meant to have a king for a father—even the king of a poor tuath had great power.

"Brian's father wants nothing to do with our tuath," she added. "He hates us all, especially my brother. It is an old war, Brian says." She sounded close to tears. Since I had never seen her cry over anything, I was astounded.

"I have been trying to think of some way to

escape," I told her. "But I can't go home."

The expression in her eyes changed and hardened. "Don't you dare."

I was stunned and I probably looked it. "Why? I can't let them take the filly away from me, and I—"

"If you infuriate him and make it harder for Brian and me to marry, I will make you sorry," she said in a low voice. I stared at her.

It was plain enough. Down deep in her angry heart, love had not improved Fallon entirely, at least not yet.

"I won't cause any trouble," I told her, and hoped it was true.

Fallon's manner softened again. She began telling me about Brian's cheerful, handsome face and how patient and kind he was with her. I nodded and kept my mouth closed on my own concerns. When she left, she ran on her way back to her Brian, no doubt worried about getting *him* in trouble if we talked too long, not me.

Walking back to the meadows, I found myself telling Dannsair about everything as usual. She listened to me intently, often lifting her head to look at me. It was as though she understood. I put one hand on her neck, and we went on that way, like friends walking side by side.

ꕥ ꕥ ꕥ

With every day that passed, I thought about what Cormac had said to me. I was desperate to know more—but how? One morning I saw the rí walking with Conall, and I ducked back into the trees, Dannsair pivoting to follow me. So. He had not left. Maybe Cormac was still here, too.

I watched the two men through the leaves, longing to hear what they were saying. Finally, I gave up and we followed our creek to a shady place where Dannsair could nap and I could stew in my own thoughts.

In the next few days, I tried twice to go uphill, toward the houses. Both times, one of the young men stopped me, asking me to lead the filly back down to the meadows below. When I said I needed to talk to Conall, they said they would tell him. But if they did, he did not come to the barn.

Then, one morning, I saw Conall and the rí standing beside the patch of woods below Gealach's enclosure. They had their backs to me, and I could see that they were lost in talk.

I knew, certain as sunrise, if I could have left the filly behind for a little while, I could circle around them and hide in the woods—and perhaps hear what they were saying.

"You wouldn't let me go alone, would you?" I asked Dannsair.

She shook her mane, probably shooing a fly, but it made me laugh. I rubbed her forehead and leaned close. "Your mother was smart and so are you."

She lifted her head sharply, her ears pricking forward. I looked up the hill to see the two men walking away, still talking. Conall saw me and he raised one hand in greeting. I gestured, hoping he would turn back to talk to me. But he did not.

I led the filly out of sight into the trees, then turned a wide circle, finding a meadow below Gealach's enclosure that was hidden by willows.

"I need to be able to walk away from you sometimes," I told her. I rubbed her forehead. "I will always come back." I pressed my forehead against hers, wishing again that she was older, that I could ride her to freedom.

Dannsair suddenly lowered her head and scented the grass. She nosed at it, then raised her head again. I wondered how many times she had done that without my noticing. Before too much longer, she would take a real interest in the grass—then she would begin to graze. And once she did, it would not be long before she was weaned. Then we would have to leave before Conall realized it.

The filly nosed at my arm, and I could tell that she was wondering why we weren't going down to the creek where I bathed and she played in the cool water as we usually did.

"Today we are going to stay here," I told her, gesturing with one hand at the little meadow. She lifted her head and her eyes followed my motion.

I did it again.

She watched again.

I walked forward and she followed. After a dozen steps, I made the motion again and said, "Stay here," the way one would talk to a baby. Then, after a moment, I walked her forward again and repeated the process.

What happened next was strange.

You might think I imagined it.

Just as I said, "Stay here," the filly hesitated in her stride. She didn't stop, but it was clear she thought *I* might stop again and she was looking out for it.

It made sense.

She thought I was her mother.

Like any foal, she had learned to stay by my side.

And why would she think I might stop? Had she learned, at least in a simple way, what "stay here" meant?

This is the truth: If we had been at home, with Bebinn and Gerroc and Tally and my little cousin Magnus and all the other people I was around each day, I would never have discovered Dannsair's ability to learn. Since I had little to do each day beyond caring for her and worrying about our escape, I passed my days seeing how much I could teach her.

It was a great deal more than I would have thought.

CHAPTER TEN

My mother has found a way for us to play together in the woods. She makes sounds that mean she is happy when I do what she wants me to do. Her voice is musical, like birds singing. I wish she could gallop faster.

Before the moon was full again, Dannsair had learned three astounding things.

First, how to stop when I told her, "Stay here."

Second—and this was much harder, believe me—she learned not to follow me after I said it. She would stand still and wait for me to turn around and walk back. Each time I went farther, often staying out of sight for a few minutes.

Third, she learned how to come when I called her name.

Don't mistake my meaning. She did not come

to me like a dog will at first. She took her time about it and sidled along, grazing, looking at me from beneath her lashes.

But I started carrying bits of my evening bread in my pockets.

She wasn't weaned, of course, and I am not sure she ever really swallowed any of the bread. But she liked the taste, and she would mouth it, working her jaw back and forth.

"What a smart filly you are," I told her over and over, rubbing her neck and her ears.

Another full moon had come and gone before I figured out how to make her canter toward me when I called.

I came upon it by accident.

One day when we were playing in the meadow, I thought I saw the dark shape of a wolf in the trees at the far end of the clearing.

"Stay here!" I said to Dannsair as I stumbled to a stop.

Then my eyes made sense of the shadows, and I laughed. It was only a misshapen lightning-stumped tree that I had seen many times. Then, by mistake, I ran again, without saying anything or making my usual hand motion for her to follow.

The filly took a single tentative step, and I realized what I had done.

"Stay there!" I called to her. She stopped and stood, watching me. I came back toward her and praised her and fed her a little bread.

We did it again. This time I walked a long ways from her, then stopped and called her name. She was uneasy being so far from me, so she trotted toward me. I turned and ran a few steps and she lunged into a gallop to catch up.

Then we tried it again.

And again.

And again.

I do not mean to make light of all the days it took to get Dannsair to understand me. But at the end of it, she would do what no horse I had ever known would do. She would stop and stand where I told her to and would wait there until I called or came back.

When I did call, she would come at a gallop.

It was amazing.

One morning, I led her downhill past her sire's enclosure. Her spirits were so high in the cool air that she galloped a little ahead, then turned back, circling me the way any foal circles its mother.

The sound of her hoofbeats had changed. The rhythmic thud was heavier now, more solid. She had grown so much. She was taller than I was now, and she could play for hours without tiring. My legs had gotten hard and muscled trying to keep up with her.

As we entered the shadows of the trees, I saw Conall and the rí walking together in a clearing ahead of us, lost in conversation.

Dannsair and I were too far away for them to have heard us—and they did not turn as I led Dannsair deeper into the woods. Then, in a little clearing, I signaled for her to stop.

She did, instantly.

"Stay here," I said quietly, making the motion with my hand. I found a place where I could see far enough through the trees to glimpse the two men. They were still talking. They had not seen me.

"Stay here," I told Dannsair a second time. I walked into the woods, then ran when I knew she could no longer see me. We had practiced this many times, and I knew she would stay—at least for a few minutes.

I cut straight through the copse of trees and then slowed and stopped, hiding behind a thick-trunked oak.

I could hear the men's voices as they came closer to me. Before long, I could make out their words.

"She'll be troublesome, I promise you that," Conall was saying. "They both will."

The rí was silent so long I was afraid that they would be out of earshot before he answered.

"The filly is all we hoped," he said, finally.

"She is," Conall said. "I saw her running with the girl a few days past. She promises to be very fast."

The rí was silent a moment. Then I heard his voice again. "The baron must be satisfied in all this. The debt must be settled."

"It will be," Conall answered.

And I could not hear another word, though I tried hard. I was afraid to get any closer. If they heard my footsteps and caught me...or if

Dannsair grew tired of waiting and whinnied or came looking for me...

Uneasy, I raced back to the filly. She was exactly where I had left her. I praised her and patted her, running the rí's words over and over in my mind.

The *baron*? Cormac had talked about a trade, a colt for a filly. I shivered. It sounded like the filly *was* Dannsair.

I led her out of the woods, then downhill and through the holly trees and the oaks to our secret meadow. Only then did I stop. "There is some trade with a Norman baron that you are part of," I told her. "So we have to leave soon."

I tried to sound steady and strong when I said it, but the truth was this: I had tried to think of a way to escape and get away without being found. I had been trying to think of where we could go besides home to my tuath. I hadn't been able to.

Dannsair tossed her head and galloped a long circle around the meadow, coming back to me with her head high and her short mane flying. Half hearted, distracted by my uneasy thoughts, I ran, then stopped. Playing as we always did,

Dannsair slid to a halt behind me, then reared. I was so lost in thought that I didn't step aside or turn and her forehoof struck my shoulder. It hurt so much that I sprawled sideways and lay in the grass for a moment. Dannsair nuzzled me gently, her breath tickling my ear.

"I am all right," I told her, feeling foolish. "I am."

I got to my feet, my shoulder aching, and led her from the meadow to the creek. We walked to the place where I usually bathed so I could soak my aching shoulder in the cool water.

Once the pain had eased, I got dressed again. My hair dripping, shivering a little, I turned to tell Dannsair that it was time to go back to the barn.

But when I faced her, I saw something that made me shiver again, fear banging against my ribs with every beat of my heart. The filly had her head down, her muzzle buried in the grass.

She was *grazing*.

CHAPTER ELEVEN

ꕥ ꕥ ꕥ

The grass tastes sweet and sour all at once. The meadows are endless, food is endless. The sun shines brighter now than it has before, the days are warmer and warmer.

You can imagine my panic.

I had hoped I would have at least another turn of the moon, another twenty-eight days or more, closer to the Feast of Samhain, before Dannsair was weaned. Now I had no time at all. Within days she was showing little interest in nursing and I had to milk the cow to keep her udder from being painfully full.

The first time Conall or the rí—or any of the boys—saw Dannsair grazing, the rí would want to take her from me. They would escort me back to the dairy byre. And I would have to go home without my filly.

That was beyond imagining. She was *mine*.

No one else loved her. None of them cared anything about her except that she was beautiful and already tall for her age and was clearly going to be a fine mare.

I knew I had to keep them from finding out that she was so close to being entirely weaned.

And I had to figure out a way to escape and where to go—both things I had spent so many days *not* figuring out.

Each day, when it got light, I led Dannsair from her stall at a trot and ran all the way to the edge of the woods. I knew if I went slower, she would lower her head to eat and someone would spot her.

Then, two or three times during the daylight hours, I led her back to the stall, as though she was hungry.

But she wasn't, not really.

With every day that passed, she was less interested in nursing and more and more interested in grazing the soft green grass from dawn to dark.

I began giving her grain to taste when she wouldn't nurse. I stood close, ready to move the pail in front of the cow if someone came in.

Before long, I began giving Dannsair a nightly meal of oats and corn. She ate both with pleasure.

Then I lay awake thinking, as I had been doing since that day in the woods.

This was the sum of my thoughts: There was no way to escape and go home without being caught. Still, my only chance was to hope they would believe I had gone home—while in fact, I was going somewhere else. It would give me a little time to find a place to hide while they searched.

I thought it might work. By the time they discovered I wasn't on my way home, we would have a few days' head start. Maybe they would guess wrong twice, or even three times, before they came the way I had gone. If we were lucky and careful, they might ride past us. I would keep to the woods. Eventually, they would have to give up looking for us to celebrate Samhain. Maybe the rí would give the baron some other filly in trade for the bay mare's colt.

Then maybe we could go home.

I knew this was all unlikely. Still, even the thinnest hope of escape lifted my heart.

I began to get ready. I put half my bread aside every day and hid it in the old yellow brat. I milked the cow empty and drank as much as I possibly could. I even made a few small rounds of unsalted cheese, using a scrubbed pail hidden in the woods to clabber the milk and a washed strip of cloth from my old brat to bind the curds.

And of course, I kept the filly hidden. Whenever we were in sight, coming and going, I ran so she would trot to keep up—and not graze.

I watched the moon like a mother hen with one chick.

We would need its light.

The night I intended to leave, the boys brought a late-bred mare into the barn, a tall black one with a beautiful face. Of course, she chose that night to have her foal. It was her first. I did not want to leave in case she needed help before the boys came to check in the morning.

It was a good thing I stayed. The mare was nervous and skittish. She had no trouble birthing her baby, but then she wanted nothing to do with it.

The poor foal lay shivering while its mother paced in a circle around it.

I waited until it stood and tried to walk toward its mother. She ignored it, switching her tail, uneasy and restless. The baby reached up to nuzzle her shoulder, and she stamped her forehoof.

That was enough for me.

I was so afraid that she would trample the newborn that I moved it into the stall with Dannsair and me. It was a colt, a little stallion. I rubbed it dry, then it lay down between us and fell asleep. I lay with my arm over the baby's shoulders, as I had once slept with Dannsair to keep her warm. I meant to wait an hour or so and put him back with his mother once she was sleepy and calmer.

And that is how Conall and the rí found me the next morning.

"What is the meaning of this?" the rí demanded.

My eyes flew open.

Conall was with him, scowling. "What have you done?" he shouted at me.

"The mare wouldn't stop pacing," I defended

myself. "She wouldn't let it nurse, and she came close to trampling it."

Conall looked stricken. The rí's face was deep red with anger.

The door opened and I saw the silhouette of a boy against the sunrise sky. As the light flooded in, I saw why they were so upset. The colt was moon-colored.

"It's beautiful," I heard a familiar voice saying.

The rí turned to face his son. "Cormac? Who gave you permission to come?"

"No one, sir," Cormac said, walking toward the stall, his eyes on the foal. "But you said if it was a colt, I could have it."

"It's a colt," I told him. Then I looked up at Conall. "Is Gealach the sire?"

Cormac grinned and I had my answer.

"He looks like Dannsair," I whispered more to myself than to anyone else. Watching the tiny foal unfold its long legs to stand up, I realized how much Dannsair had grown, how tall and strong she had become.

A rustling sound made me turn, and I saw Dannsair nosing at the oats in the bottom of the cow's bucket. A sheen of cold sweat broke on my forehead.

"Look at that," the rí said lightly. "She is eating on her own."

Conall frowned at me. "How long since she began?"

I tried to look puzzled and surprised. "I am not sure I have ever seen her do that before," I lied.

But Dannsair was working her way across the bottom of the bucket, her jaws moving in a rhythm that shouted out to anyone in the world that this was not the first time she had tasted oats.

There was no place else to look, so I looked at Cormac. He met my eyes and we stood awkwardly, staring at each other.

"Let's see if the mare will take her foal now," Conall said quietly. He came into the stall and picked up the newborn.

"If she won't, the cow would feed him, I think," I said quietly. No one answered me, but Cormac shot me a grateful look. He hadn't thought of that. All too often, a foal whose mother will not care for it is doomed to die.

I studied Cormac's face as he watched Conall carry the colt to its mother. I knew how he felt. This was his colt and he already loved it.

The rí stepped around Conall to open the stall gate.

I held my breath.

The mare was still nervous, and the men approaching the stall gate didn't help. But once her foal was with her, and Conall was out, she stopped pacing. We all stood in silence as the baby sidled closer, swaying on his long legs. He reached upward to nurse. The mare stood still, her ears twitching. Then she turned to nuzzle the baby's back as he ate his first meal.

"I am so glad," I whispered to Cormac after the foal had been suckling for a few minutes.

He grinned at me again.

I was so relieved.

If the foal's mother had not wanted him—what would I have done? It was my fault they had been separated so long—I hadn't meant to fall asleep.

Cormac kept glancing at me, then back at the foal. He looked so happy. It pleased me to know that one day he would have this colt that looked so much like Dannsair. He would be kind to it, I was sure.

"The baron will be glad to see this one," the rí said from behind us. I spun around to see him sliding a leather halter onto Dannsair's muzzle. Her head was up, her eyes wide.

"Leave it on," he told me. "It's time she got used to it."

Conall met my eyes for an instant. "I will begin training the filly as soon as she is fully weaned."

I nodded, lowering my eyes.

"I will be careful with her," Conall said to me.

"Enough," the rí said. "I see no reason to discuss anything with this girl."

He turned then and walked fast, leading the way out. Conall followed and did not look back, but Cormac did, a glance as quick as a sparrow's wing.

Then they were all gone.

CHAPTER TWELVE

ஐ ஐ ஐ

My mother is frightened. I don't know what scares her. I scent no wolves. I know she will protect me, whatever the danger is. She always has.

I began to gather my things, thinking furiously. I had been wrong to believe I'd have another turn of the moon, that I could hide the fact that Dannsair was almost eating on her own. Now I had no time at all, perhaps not even the rest of this day.

"Larach?"

The voice came from outside the door, and I ran to lie down and pretended to be asleep.

I heard the door open as Dannsair lowered her head to nuzzle the back of my neck.

"Larach?"

I opened my eyes when I was sure of the voice. "Cormac? What is it?"

He opened the stall gate. "My father has promised Dannsair to the Baron of Athenry in trade for the bay mare's colt."

I sat up and Dannsair stirred, then rolled onto her chest, her eyes still soft with sleep.

"I know," I told him, trying to still my heart. "I overheard them talking one day." I forced myself to look sad, as though I knew I had to give her up. Cormac had been kind to me, but I was not foolish enough to think that he would not tell his father if he suspected that I was about to run away with Dannsair.

Cormac stepped back as Dannsair stood and shook herself. "I hope one day we will meet," he said quietly. "Each of us riding a moon-colored horse."

I was afraid to react. It sounded as though he knew exactly what I was planning. "I saw Fallon from a distance a few days past," I said, keeping my voice even. "Will you tell her I wish her well?"

"I will," he answered, and I hoped he would. I

wanted to say some kind of good-bye to Fallon. Mean as she had always been to me, and as little as she thought about me now, she was a big part of my home, my life. Once I left here, it was possible that I would never see her again.

Cormac was looking at me intently. "She has charmed my brother."

I nodded cautiously. "I have seen them."

"If they marry," he said, "our fathers will have to talk, not fight."

"But would they talk, even then?"

He shrugged. "Maybe. Or they will fight harder," he admitted. "I hope not."

"Why are they enemies?" I asked him.

He sighed. "My forefathers fought with O'Connor two hundred years past. Yours did not."

I looked at him. "Two hundred years?"

He looked aside, at the ground. "My father does not forget these things. Nor does yours. And your father did steal the gray mare during a battle with the Normans."

I bit my lip. "He told me he found her."

Cormac looked at the ground. "Perhaps he did, but he knew whose she was."

"He said he didn't," I told him. Then I softened my voice. "But I am a girl. He doesn't talk to me about these things. I wish I were a boy," I added, without knowing I was going to say it.

Cormac's eyebrows arched. "Why? To fight?"

I shook my head. "No. So I could stay here and work with the horses."

"You are good with them," he said. Then he gestured with one hand to include the barns, the walled fields, the meadows on the hill. "My father is breeding good horses here. Every tuath, every castle lord will want them for his men to ride."

I instinctively put my arm over Dannsair's withers. I did not want to imagine her bleeding from a sword wound, wandering, as weak and scared as her mother had been when my father brought her limping home. I saw Cormac glance at the stall where his moon-colored foal was sleeping next to its mother now.

"It's getting light. You must go before they miss you," I whispered.

"Yes," Cormac answered. "Here." From the folds of his brat he pulled out a water flask made of deerskin. I took it and he smiled. "And this."

I watched him walk to the end of the aisle, bending to reach behind the wooden boxes that held the oats and corn. He pulled out a cloak and gave it to me.

It was brown and gray, mottled like oak bark, large enough to sleep beneath, and made of thick warm wool. I had never seen such a garment except on nobility.

"Thank you," I managed, knowing now that he understood everything. He knew I was leaving, that I would be chased. He had even thought to give me a plain-colored cloak—so the color would not mark me as a thief when anyone got close enough to see my soiled leine and bare feet.

Cormac held my glance another moment. "There is a path at the bottom of the hill," he said. "It leads north into the forest."

I nodded.

He said no more as he turned and left. I stared after him until he closed the door. Then I did what I had rehearsed in my mind a hundred times.

First, I made sure the gold pin was secure inside my brat.

Then I gathered all I had saved—the bread, my little rounds of cheese, the small piece of a bronze blade I had found. I wrapped everything in my old yellow brat and tied the bundle with the strips of cloth I had used to press the cheese.

I carried half a bucket of corn and oats to the cow and kissed her on her kind muzzle and thanked her and bid her farewell. Conall would keep her, I was sure. If he ever had another orphaned foal, she would likely let it nurse. I closed the stall gate carefully so she would not wander. I let Dannsair out and gave her oats and corn, knowing that it might be the last she saw of either one for a long time.

I put the water flask's strap over my shoulder, then wrapped myself in the wondrous cloak. Warmth settled on my shoulders and down my back beneath the thick cloth. I took the leather halter off Dannsair and hung it on the stall gate.

I would not be called a thief and have it be true.

Once we were outside, and far enough from the buildings so that Dannsair's hoofbeats would not be heard, I ran.

Dannsair cantered beside me, breaking back into a trot when she found herself getting ahead.

We reached the base of the long hill, and I stood, my heart thudding in my chest. I knew, more or less, how to go back to the town we had come through, and from there, I was sure I could find the river crossing.

The idea of going home pulled at me, and brought tears to my eyes. But it was a simple fact: I couldn't.

I started off, turning to follow the path that led into the forest. I ran, but slower, a pace I knew I could sustain for a long time. Dannsair cantered, then trotted, then cantered again, matching her strides to mine as she always did.

The morning air was cool and damp, and there was a fog lying along the ground. I shivered and pulled my brat closer, beneath the cloak. I touched the little gold pin on the underside of the cloth.

It was a comfort at first. Then it made me feel homesick again. I was running away from Bebinn and Gerroc and my mother and everyone else I loved.

"You would love little Magnus," I told Dannsair as we ran. Thinking about my cousin brought new tears to my eyes. What if I never saw any of my family again?

The path started uphill, and I ran as long as I could, then dropped back to a walk. The sun was up behind the clouds now, and my spirits lifted.

Dannsair had slowed with me, but I could tell she didn't want to. She pranced, tossing her head and switching her tail.

"Get big enough to carry me," I told her. "Then you won't have to wait for me."

She blew out a breath, shaking her mane. I remembered when it was so short it stood straight up. Now it fell along her neck. Soon it would be a moon-silver cascade. The time that had passed since I had left the tuath felt very short—and very long, both at once.

We kept on uphill, following the narrow path. Then, just as we reached the crest, I heard something. Before I could react, riders came over the hill. They wore the bright-colored clothing of royalty, their cloaks long and full enough to drape backward over their horses' tails.

"Look, Father," a boy cried out. "They've sent a serving maid with the filly. That's her, isn't it? The same color as Gealach!"

A man with long white hair reined in his horse to stare at me. "I am the Baron of Athenry. Where are the others? Conall, at least, should be with you. And why is there no rope on the horse, no halter?"

"I am sorry we are late," a man's voice rang out.

Stunned, I turned to see Conall galloping up the hill with two riders behind him. Cormac was one of them. The other boy I did not know.

I fought tears, swiping angrily at my eyes.

How could I have been so careless? I had assumed we had a few days, perhaps much longer. Conall had talked about training the filly soon. I stared at him, but he did not meet my eyes. The answer was simple, then. He had meant to fool me.

And had Cormac meant to betray me as well, with his advice on what path to take? I looked at him and his eyes were full of agony. If he had known he was sending me into the path of the baron this morning, he wasn't at ease with the betrayal at least.

My whole body was trembling with fury and fear. We could not escape. The riders would run us down. I could not keep them from taking Dannsair from me. There were too many of them.

I put my arm across Dannsair's back and tried to think. I had no friend here. Cormac had his own family to look to, his own honor to preserve. And what help could he give me now?

As Conall and the boys reined in, placing themselves in a triad around me and Dannsair, Cormac glanced at me, then at Conall, who was greeting the baron, then back.

"I didn't know," he whispered to me. Then he lifted his voice and faced the Normans. "We thought you would be coming from the southeast as usual, sir, until my father told us you'd been to the sea."

The baron nodded.

"Isn't she a beauty?" Cormac asked, gesturing to Dannsair. "This girl has cared for her very well."

Laughter broke out at that. I realized that there were even more riders than I had thought. Some were blurred by the fog.

"You allow girls to care for warhorses?" the baron demanded. "I hope she hasn't made the destrier soft and silly."

They all laughed again.

"The girl has done us all a great service," Conall said. "The gray mare died in foaling, but she saved the filly."

The baron frowned and leaned forward in his saddle. "My mare is dead?"

Conall nodded somberly. "No one's fault, sire. She had the best of care, but was stolen from us. When we found the filly, she was already gone. The rí asked me to tell you that there are three fine Norseblood foals and a yearling mare he will bring you in payment for the mare as soon as the foals can travel."

The baron was silent and no one else dared speak. Finally he sat back in his saddle. "I am very sorry to know that mare is gone. Horses that finely bred rarely come to us here in the wildlands of Eire."

Conall nodded. "We are all distraught, sir. As you must recall, her second foal sired by Gealach was to be ours to keep."

The baron was looking at Dannsair, his head tilted like any horseman looking at a fine weanling.

Conall cleared his throat. "The rí is eager to see you, sir."

The Baron of Athenry made a face like a petulant child. "I am angered about the mare, and I have been far from home for a fortnight. We will come again before Samhain." He gestured at Dannsair and looked at me. "Did you bring a halter?"

I couldn't react. Conall nodded and pulled the one I had left behind from beneath his cloak. I couldn't do anything but watch as he put it on Dannsair, then fastened a leather line to the iron ring.

I knew I could call Dannsair and she would fight to come to me. Maybe she could break free, but then what? We could not outrun them, and she could easily be hurt as they chased us down.

I stared as one of the riders took the lead and

gently turned Dannsair around. He pulled her toward him as he mounted his horse again. He rode forward a little.

As soon as Dannsair realized that the rope forced her to follow the stranger's horse, she wrenched around, rearing, whickering wildly at me.

It made the riders laugh again, to see her so frantic.

I hated them all.

Every one.

Even Cormac.

Especially Cormac. He had told me about this path. Even if he had meant no harm, he had caused this. I might have gone a different way if he hadn't told me.

The baron and his men turned around. Conall and the two boys watched as they rode off. Dannsair whinnied frantically, trying to turn back to me. The men rode closer, boxing her in so that she couldn't see me at all.

My eyes streamed with tears as I stood there, numb and shaking.

Conall slid off his horse and came closer. "I am sorry, Larach," he whispered. "Come back to the barns. You can wait for Fallon and Brian to decide whether they will defy the rí and your father or not. Or I will take you back to the dairy byre. But the filly is the business of the rí and the baron. You cannot interfere."

I faced him. "Leave me alone."

He patted my shoulder, then mounted his horse.

I heard Cormac say something.

"Leave me alone!" I shouted without turning. "I'll come back when I am ready to come back."

I could hear their horses moving, could hear them talking in low voices. Conall said something and the boys quieted. Then they cantered down the path. I did not turn to watch them leaving.

Go back to the barns?

I would *not*.

I would rescue Dannsair, no matter how long it took. She would not be doomed to a life of battles and pain.

Not so long as I was alive.

I tightened the cloak around my shoulders and began to walk, following the sound of hoofbeats through the fog.